James A Cooper

Table of Contents

James A Cooper

Foreword

I have never written a book before. So why write one now? I'm not sure I can give a completely satisfactory answer, but I'll try.

Before I start explaining myself, I should recognize a few people whose support helped me make this possible. First, my wife Kathy, for not only putting up with my desire to do this, but helping edit; and second, my brother John for helping proofread the manuscript. Both provided feedback that I needed to finish this project up, and I thank both of you for that.

To get back to why I decided to write a book now... I grew up consuming pulp adventure novels, and they always ignited my imagination. As a boy I could not read enough of the works of Edgar Rice Burroughs, H. Rider Haggard, or Sir Arthur Conan Doyle, especially ones like *John Carter of Mars*, *The Lost World*, *King Solomon's Mines*, *Doc Savage* novels, anthologies like *Adventure Stories for Boys,* and any other books that fell into similar genres. I also consumed Tolkien, and a number of other Sci-Fi writers. I should mention that not all of my favorite books were fiction (*The Rivers Ran East*, for instance). With the exception of Middle-Earth, none of those stories or worlds really stuck in my gut the same way as the old-school adventure stories above.

Second, Most of those stories were written in or about another time, when the world seemed much bigger, and less explored and exploited. I fell in love with this idea that there is always a new frontier, an undiscovered country, or ancient lost city that needs to be explored. That idea also had a lot to do with many of my choices in life. I like to get out in the world, and thankfully, I've managed to see and do a few things. In fact, my experiences have convinced me that there is more to the world, and ultimately to *us*, than we see on the surface of our modern society.

At some point, all of the stories and experiences that I've consumed started to boil up to the surface. The root ideas of this story go back to my boyhood, but it was not brought to the surface until I had some life experience under my belt. I had a story forming in my head, and I decided it was time to get it out.

This particular idea has been lurking in the back of my mind since I was a teenager, and it is time to give it some voice. It would occasionally surface and evolve a little bit more each time, until I finally realized a life-long dream and visited the Middle East, in particular Egypt, Jordan and Israel. That trip provided a few key missing pieces to help tie some of the story ideas together. Climbing Jebel Al-Mahdbah, seeing the ancient worship complex with my own eyes, and reading some of the lesser-known ideas about its origins helped bring it together for me.

So I used that extra little bit of inspiration, and attempted to write an adventure story of my own. I wanted the medium to be one I was familiar with. The same kind of stories and novels that I loved as a boy seemed like the perfect vehicle; an old-fashioned pulp adventure story.

I see this as a bit of an homage to all of those books, stories and movies that inspired me. I do not pretend to think this is terribly good. It is, however, mine. And it is a story I want to tell, so I like it. And if others like it well enough, there may be more stories that follow. I'll let you decide whether or not I succeeded.

Jim Cooper
Marysville, Ohio
2021
For my family

James A Cooper

The
COVENANT
STONE

From The Adventures of Buck Haggard

James A Cooper

Prologue

Emmitt Carter looked up at the two obelisk-shaped stone pillars above him. His sense of urgency was at an all-time high, adrenaline rushing through his veins. Recent events had kept him on the run for the last forty-eight hours, and in spite of his sixty years Emmitt felt more energized than tired. Emmitt knew he benefited from an active life, but before two days ago, he never imagined that he would be in a race for an object that could change the world.

Emmitt was certain his pursuers were close behind. He arrived in the nearby Arab town earlier this morning, and had scrambled to find a donkey to aid his ascent up the steep mountain side. Despite how he felt at the moment, Emmitt knew the pace of the last few days and lack of sleep would catch up to him soon.

This was not the first time he had been here, but he now believed this place to be even more important to the historical record than he had ever imagined. Sixteen years ago, in the summer of 1930, he had visited this place with his teenage daughter Kate. At that time, he was investigating theories that this mountain had played a key role in Biblical history; he now understood he was barely scratching the surface, although there was much he still didn't grasp yet.

That trip also inspired his daughter to not only study history, but also become an expert in ancient written languages. In fact, Kate's expertise made her an invaluable partner and contributor to Emmitt's research.

For the second time, his research into the roots of ancient civilizations had led him to this unlikely, isolated mountaintop in the Middle East. If he had correctly interpreted the clues in his recent search, this location held the key to an extremely valuable artifact, one that could change history – and might also be priceless, although that was not his motivation. Unfortunately, others were very interested in the potential value of this prize.

Emmitt had started his research as a purely academic pursuit, for the sake of expanding mankind's understanding of his own beginnings. Emmitt was unusual in this regard – he pursued knowledge with the belief that it should be openly shared. He saw more value in knowledge and education than in objects and wealth. Too many of his colleagues preferred to profit from their work first, and share the knowledge later. Emmitt had no such inclination, so he often openly discussed his projects.

A result of this was that news of his latest research reached some surprising people. On more than one occasion, he was approached with offers to privately fund or purchase his research. Emmitt was uncomfortable with accepting money from private parties for the work he did. Emmitt did not want to be indebted to any private party when it came to his research. He believed that could only undermine the objectivity of his work, and limit his ability to share it with the world.

The first offer was to fund, and consequently obtain all rights to, his research. The man who made the offer had visited only a few weeks prior. He gave Emmitt a bad feeling as soon as he walked in the door.

The man was a large, solidly built German with black hair and a faint scar on his left cheek. He introduced himself as Mr. Wilhelm Weiss. He was accompanied by two men, introduced as Dieter and Karl. Their mannerisms were very disciplined and formal, and suggested recent military service. The assistants contributed nothing to the conversation, but their presence did foster a sense of intimidation.

The Second World War had recently ended, and anti-German sentiment was common in the United States. In spite of this, Emmitt resisted the urge to judge the man because of his nationality, but he could not deny these men were clearly prior military. The implied Nazi associations were too difficult for Emmitt to ignore.

Emmitt passed on their very lucrative offer. The Germans were clearly upset; Mr. Weiss maintained a cordial manner, but his expression betrayed his anger. He also managed to make a few veiled threats to Emmitt's reputation. Emmitt asked his daughter to call the local police, which prompted the three visitors to leave. Emmitt was convinced he had made the right choice.

The second offer was different. A man claiming to be from Armenia made an offer to buy him out and take over all present research, again, for a very generous amount of money. The man that made the offer walked away disappointed but gracious.

He also left Emmitt with an offer to help if he should find himself in any difficult situations. Emmitt chalked this encounter up to a competitor, certainly dubious, but without underlying nefarious intent. Little did he know that he would be working with that 'competitor' today.

The midday sun was heating the arid mountain top to a sweltering ninety-eight degrees. Emmitt wiped the sweat from his forehead as he looked around to make sure he had not been followed up the mountain.

Now that he had returned to this spot, the stakes could not be higher. Emmitt knew he might fail, but he had to try to recover the artifact before it was too late. The risk of failure was great enough that he had left clues for Kate. If he failed to recover the artifact, Emmitt knew she could pick up the trail. He just hoped she wouldn't decide to run off on her own. She was stubborn enough to do that, even though Emmitt left instructions in case anything should happen.

He steered to a flat sandy area at the top of the ridge ahead. The weather beaten obelisks sat on a man-made plateau just above to his left, and a faint trail let up a taller, second peak to his right. He dismounted and tied his donkey off to a small shrub at the top of the ridge.

Emmitt grabbed his shoulder bag and set off for the plateau. The massive stone pillars marked the area that he needed to search. While visiting this site sixteen years ago, he saw them as a fascinating monument with possible historical connections to the Old Testament. Now he realized they may mark clues to one of the most powerful objects in the world.

As he hiked up the rocky slope to the plateau, a familiar figure stepped out from behind the nearest pillar. The man's tan face was accentuated by the scar on his cheek. His eyes flashed as he smiled – a cold, evil smile. His sharp German accent echoed across the plateau. "Hello, Professor. I think you should have accepted my offer."

Emmitt stopped and took a deep breath. He had planned for this, but hoped it would not be necessary. Now it was up to Kate. He just hoped she could find the right person to help.

Chapter 1 - Quito - Ecuador

Henry James Haggard was tired. Not physically tired, but mentally weary. He adjusted his weather-beaten, blue and red 1939 Cincinnati Reds baseball cap to keep the midday sun out of his eyes. He was wearing a worn, off-white linen shirt with sleeves rolled up to his elbows, and khaki pants that had seen more than a few excursions into the jungle. A pair of old army-issued boots had seen better days. Haggard felt like his name had finally caught up with him.

As he walked the dusty streets of Quito, he tried to shake the feeling with no success. He was on the way to meet a client, and he needed to be mentally sharp or lose the business. His mind began to drift, and he reflected on his life since the War. Haggard was slowly realizing he needed something more.

Captain Henry "Buck" Haggard ended his OSS career in 1945 while investigating possible Nazi escape routes into South America. He was never satisfied that his superiors took it seriously, and the few leads he had uncovered were largely ignored. It was clear that the OSS and the American government wanted to move on, and his last months in the service had left him disillusioned. Buck's partner shared many of the same sentiments, so they both decided to resign their commissions.

Jock Howard had been Buck's best friend and right hand man since the early days of the War. They served together in the OSS, and proved to be an effective team in several wartime intelligence missions. They were assigned to investigate Nazi Rat Lines into South America in May of 1945. When Buck decided to leave the service, Jock followed.

Buck had saved enough cash to buy a surplus Army aircraft, a Grumman G-21 Goose. The Grumman aircraft had enabled Buck and Jock to become mobile over the entire western half of the Amazon basin, and was essential to their operation. Soon the two of them had set up shop in Ecuador, working as guides for hunting, exploration (and occasionally less reputable jobs) that required trips into the Amazon.

Both men could fly and operate the plane with ease; Buck typically took the stick, while Jock was a gifted mechanic. Their background in the Army OSS and experiences in the War had prepared them for life in a place frequented by mercenaries and cutthroats. The Goose, as they affectionately called it, along with their collective experience, opened up a door to clients they could not have taken on otherwise.

Their usual clientele tended to range from honest scientists trying to expand the bounds of natural science to the fringe explorers and treasure hunters looking for remnants of lost civilizations. The former were easy clients; they knew their limitations, and accepted that Buck and Jock knew the rain forest better than they ever would. The latter were a little more common, and typically needed to be reined in.

It seemed like a lot of rich, bored Americans and Brits found their way to Ecuador and Peru in order to make a name by finding some version of El Dorado or claiming to have evidence of some unknown, legendary treasure.

Buck had no use for fairy tales, but had been more than happy to guide them into the jungle until they either gave up or found something that they believed was of value. As long as the paycheck was there, Buck and his partner were willing and able to take the job.

Now a year after the fall of Berlin, Buck found his current lifestyle unfulfilling. Only recently, Buck had started to realize that he wasn't in it for the money as much as he was searching for something. Buck was slowly realizing he needed something more. He just wasn't sure what. Lately Buck had started to feel like he needed a purpose; his early years in the military had never failed to provide that. But something was missing now, and Buck just couldn't put a finger on what it was.

As Buck neared his destination, he thought about their last job. He and Jock had just returned from an exploratory expedition in the South American interior the previous night. It turned out to be a failure, not only for their customer, but a financial bust for them.

16

This client was a Brit, one of the rich, bored types that seemingly had money to burn. He paid half up front, and agreed to pay the remainder after the expedition. The old man was looking for some lost plateau that he thought would contain treasure – of course, it was a dead end. No treasure, just long, hot, sweaty days in the jungle until the customer had had enough.

Buck knew the trip would be a wild goose chase from the beginning, but as long as the customer was paying, he was willing to guide and protect him. In this case, the old man refused to pay the remainder of the fee after returning, claiming failure was as much Buck's fault as his. In the end, Buck and his partner fell short of covering their expenses.

Despite the weariness he felt, Buck was motivated to land a good job quick, to make up for the losses of the last one.

Buck approached Mosley's Cantina, a place frequented by very few respectable or law-abiding people. Most of the people in Mosley's were either looking for something, or selling something that couldn't be found in other places. It was here that Buck and his partner usually met and evaluated their potential clients.

Buck entered through the saloon-style doors and looked around for Jock. His eyes slowly adjusted to the dim lighting. Ceiling fans kept the hot air moving, providing some relief from the South American heat.

He saw Jock seated at a table in the back corner, wearing a tan short sleeve shirt. His broad, six-foot-five frame and red hair was impossible to miss. To Buck's surprise, Jock had company – female company. Her back was to Buck. As he made his way toward them, Buck noted shoulder-length brown hair pulled back in a ponytail. Buck could also see she wasn't dressed like a tourist; khaki shirt with sleeves rolled up to her elbows, brown equestrian riding pants tucked into a pair of well-cared-for black riding boots. A dark brown leather satchel was on the floor beside her chair. Buck decided she must be here on business.

Good, he thought, we could use the work. Maybe we'll make up for the last job.

Buck heard Jock say "Here he is now" as he approached. Buck stood facing the woman. She was definitely attractive, but did not look like she was worried about impressing anyone with her looks. She didn't have to. Her natural beauty needed no makeup to enhance it, and she wore none. In another situation, he might have reacted by offering to buy her a drink. Today, she was a potential client. She was here on business, and so was he.

The woman looked him in the eye, extended her hand and said, "You must be Mr. Haggard." Buck shook her hand, nodding to acknowledge her statement. She continued with no hesitation,

"Mr. Haggard, my name is Kate Carter. I was just telling your associate that I believe I require your services on a very urgent matter." She paused, and then added, "You come highly recommended, and I need the best."

Buck sat down and said "I appreciate that, but who sent you our way? No offense, but you don't look like our typical customer. Where exactly did you hear about us?" Buck wanted the work, but he also needed to make sure they weren't going to waste time and effort like the last job.

Kate took a breath. "Very well - a man named Leonard Clark, who sometimes frequents this part of the world, gave me your name. He tells me you were one of the best OSS agents he knew during the war, and that you are ideally suited for the kind of help I require."

That name got his attention. "How do you know Len?" Buck asked.

"He and my father did some work together during the war. My father, Emmitt Carter, consulted for the Army on one or two occasions. He told me that that Leonard Clark should be the first person I should ask for help. When I approached Mr. Clark, he gave me your name. He was especially adamant you were the person I should ask once I provided the details of my problem. Apparently, you have a reputation for getting things done."

Kate looked Buck in the eye, "Which brings me to why I am here. My father is missing, and I need help locating him."

Buck sat back. "I'm not sure I understand why. Len knows this part of the world every bit as well – Hell, probably better – than we do. He's been all over this side of South America. If your father is lost in the jungle anywhere between here and Brazil –"

Kate interrupted. "I never said he was lost in the jungle, Mr. Haggard. My father disappeared in the Middle East, somewhere between Palestine and Transjordan. I have been told you spent considerable time in the Middle East during the War."

"Actually some of it was in Europe, but I did spend a lot of time in North Africa, and made it up through Transjordan once or twice." Buck said. He added, "Listen Lady, just to be up front, I spent the first half of the war picking sand out of my boots, and I've got no burning desire to go back to that part of the world. What's more, that is a long ways away, and I'm not sure you can afford us, especially for a trip like that."

Jock, who had been quiet up till now, spoke. "Maybe you should hear her out Buck. Based on what I've heard so far, she really needs our help. I've only got part of the story, so we need to back up and fill you in on what Ms. Carter needs from us. "

Buck sat back in his chair. "OK, let's hear it. But fair warning, you're going to have to give me a pretty good reason to take this job."

Kate took a breath. "OK. I need to give you some background, just so you have the full picture. I'm looking for my father, but there may be more at stake."

"My father is a professor at Barnett University in upstate New York. He teaches ancient world history and runs their archeological research programs. Several years ago, he started to piece together a theory that the world's oldest civilizations had a single predecessor – An advanced, unknown civilization that somehow passed on knowledge to the Egyptians, Sumerians, perhaps even ancient South Americans. I specialize in ancient languages, so I've been helping him in this research.

"Over the last six months, Dad uncovered references to something that may have been of great significance to this antediluvian civilization, and may be of even great value today.

19

Buck interrupted, "Antediluvian – you mean predating Noah's flood?"

Kate said "Yes. Clearly, any civilization that predates known history would have to extend back beyond the supposed flood. In fact, the "flood" as we call it may have been the motivation for these people to pass their knowledge on to the Sumerians, Egyptians, and others."

Buck interrupted her again. "So I take it that you believe that this research is why he is missing." It was a statement, not a question.

"That's right, Kate continued. "I think his research has gained the attention of several groups of people, and at least one of them has sinister intentions. But first I think you will need a little more background. I'll try not to bore you with too much detail."

Her tone conveyed that she was used to dealing with people who were less educated than herself. Buck picked up on this, and half smiling said "Don't worry doll, I'm not bored – yet"

Kate ignored his jab and went on. "Dad's research uncovered evidence of what can only be described as an ancient device, possible some kind of power source – one that is either powerful enough to change our world for the better, or so destructive that in the wrong hands, it could make the last war all for nothing.

"Dad was searching for the location of this object in Palestine when we last heard from him. Shortly after his scheduled arrival in the Dead Sea area, I received a package from him. It was his notebook, with no accompanying letter or explanation. Just a bookmark on the pages that pertain to his research in the Dead Sea area, and a note scribbled in the margins telling me to contact Mr. Clark right away."

Buck stopped her. "So let's take first thing first. I take it you think you know who is responsible? Your comments suggest you at least have some strong suspicions, am I right?"

"Yes," Kate answered. "Before he left, he was visited twice – first by three men with German accents, and then a few days later by another man who may have been from the Near East – Turkey perhaps. I'm really not sure about his nationality.

"The first visitors offered to buy his research. Dad refused to sell, and they became very pushy. They left after he threatened to have me call the police. The second visit was different. This man seemed genuinely worried that Dad was putting himself or others at risk. When he left, he asked Dad to stop before it was too late. After the Germans, we really weren't sure if it was meant as a threat or a well-intentioned warning."

Jock looked at Buck. He was already familiar with this part of the story, having heard it just before Buck arrived. He wanted Buck to take this in. "Let's take this in order - Tell us more about the Germans" Jock said. "Anything you can remember is potentially useful."

Buck listened intently as Kate continued "There were three of them. I answered the door when they arrived, so I did get a good look at them.

"Their appearance and how they carried themselves stood out - They were dressed conservatively, in business suits, and seemed very formal and well-groomed."

"How did you know they were German? " Buck asked. "Did they tell you, or did you hear them speak it?"

"No, they didn't tell me – and only one spoke in front of me. His accent was clearly German. He seemed to be the leader of the group."

Buck raised his eyebrows "What told you that?"

"The others clearly deferred to him. He spoke for them, and they seemed to hang back and to either side of him. Almost as if they were subservient to him. When they entered my father's study, they waited for him to enter first. When they left I noticed the same sort of deference to him. They clearly worked for him, but this seemed almost extreme. It struck me as military in nature."

Buck shot a glance at Jock, "Son of a Bitch – Nazis..." he muttered. Jock nodded in agreement.

Kate scanned their faces for a moment. "You can't be serious – this is in upstate New York - And the war ended a year ago! Besides, what would Nazis want with Dad's research?"

Buck leaned forward. "Hitler had a thing for relics – This was an ongoing obsession with him. He believed that he was leading the world into a new age. His inner circle all believed that obtaining ancient relics could supposedly give him some sort of supernatural edge over his opponents. I've heard rumors of him sending his goons to find religious artifacts since the 1930s.

"I worked with an Intel officer who apparently had a couple run-ins with this activity before the War. He never said much, except that the Nazis failed both times. We knew Hitler's men found other priceless – although in my opinion useless – artifacts on a number of other occasions.

"As far as your surprise that Nazis could surface now, in New York, or anywhere else, don't be. They hide everywhere, often in plain sight. The rat lines out of Germany extended all over free Europe and into both North and South America. In fact, that's how we ended up here. My last assignment in the OSS was to trace out South American rat lines, but we really didn't achieve much before I resigned.

"All the same, we know they're here in South America - and from here they can get to just about anywhere else in the world without much trouble. There have even been rumors that our government took on some of their engineers and scientists, if you can believe that."

Kate digested this for a moment. "So does this mean you believe my father was a target for *Nazis* because of his research? Why?"

Buck responded "I believe this because of my experience with chasing the rat lines – escape routes – from Germany into South America. Many of Hitler's advisors who weren't captured have been coming here to start planning ahead for their fourth Reich. I don't believe they can muster the resources to come back, but they certainly want to.

"And it seems to me that your fathers' research may fit in with their plans in one of two ways: first, some the Nazi inner circle held the belief that they can master the world using supernatural resources or weapons; second, and this is more practical, they probably need to raise cash. There are a lot of people out there that will pay well for ancient artifacts.

"What else do you recall about these goons? Anything, looks, odd mannerisms, anything we can use may end up being useful"

Kate thought for a moment. "The leader was taller, and dark-haired. The other two had blonde hair. They were average height, around five-ten to six feet tall. The leader was larger, and seemed pretty imposing, I would say at least six foot five. He had a faint scar on his left cheek. That's about all I can remember about their appearances."

Buck's expression went cold. "Krause," he muttered.

"Not good," Jock added.

Kate looked back and forth between the two men. "He said his name was Weiss, but I doubted his sincerity – it didn't seem to be a strong point. Do you know him?"

Buck spoke "If I'm right, yes. Wilhelm Krause was a Nazi SS Officer that I had a few run-ins with during the war. He's smart, nasty and ruthless. I don't want to alarm you, but if he is involved, your father is in real danger."

"I already assumed his life is at stake," Kate said. "But what makes this man so dangerous?"

"He was one of Himmler's elite – This guy specialized in obtaining items that had some sort of religious or supernatural meaning to the Nazis." Buck paused, "I didn't think he made out of Berlin. By some accounts, he was in the bunker with Hitler."

Jock jumped into the conversation. "Buck, you know those Russian reports were never that reliable. We were never 100% sure what actually happened in that bunker or who was there when the Russians found it – but we are sure that a lot of top Nazi brass got out of Berlin at the last minute. Krause could have easily escaped."

Buck looked at his partner. "Yeah, no question it's possible". He turned his attention back to Kate. "Ok, so next thing – I am wondering why your father's research into some mythological artifact got this kind of attention – Even The Fuehrer's goons wanted to make sure they were looking for a real object vs chasing a myth. What got their attention?"

Kate resisted the urge to become defensive. "I never said it was a myth, I said my father found evidence – meaning both real-world indications as well as documentation in ancient texts – that indicate the real possibility of an artifact that could be very powerful, if there is any truth to the legends he was researching. Of course, the real proof is in finding the object – but there are indications that it is – or was - a very real thing."

"Ok, I get that ancient documents, scrolls or what-have-you, could mention some sort of magical object, but that's nothing new or impressive – what is the 'real-world' evidence you are talking about?"

Kate reached for the bag next to her chair. She brought out a small oblong wooden box about 12 inched long and eight inches wide and high. Kate slowly opened the box.

As Buck and Jock leaned forward to see, she warned them "Be careful – you can pick it up, but handle it gently."

Inside was a translucent crystalline object. Buck couldn't be sure if it was simply reflecting ambient light, or actually emitting a very slight blue-white glow. The object was 10 inches long, six inches wide at one end and narrowed to about a three inch apex at the other. Its total thickness was about three inches. The outline reminded Buck of a squat, bulky obelisk. It had no inner structure or components that he could see.

"What is that?' Jock asked. "Is it fragile?" His hand was only inches from the box.

"No, it's exceptionally solid, and it is very old. Dad and I aren't really sure how old. At first, we thought the obelisk-like shape suggested Egyptian origin, but we really can't find anything in its immediate design or construction that relates it back to any known historical civilization. In fact, we believe it predates known history. Dad found this because he was investigating his theory, following clues he found in ancient texts describing keys to a powerful talisman or relic hidden for thousands of years. The texts describe a pair of objects - crystal keystones - used to unlock and control a powerful talisman, and this fits the description of one of the keystones.

"Dad found it in Palestine, in a complex of caves near the Dead Sea. In fact, he was looking for the companion piece when he disappeared."

Kate explains her father's research

She hesitated, observing their reactions. "You can pick it up, but be careful. It's not really the crystal I'm concerned about. It's the reaction you may have." She swept her gaze from Jock to Buck as she spoke. "Just trust me and touch it gently – you will see what I mean."

Jock cautiously put his hand on the object, and suddenly pulled it back in surprise. "What the hell…!"

"What is it?' Buck asked.

Jock rubbed his hand. "It's kind of like putting your hand on a live wire – it didn't really hurt, but you could feel a sort current running over the surface. That's as close as I can get to describing it"

Kate spoke, "Had you grabbed it more aggressively, the reaction would have been stronger. It's almost as if this object reacts to how it's handled. We still haven't figured out how it stores this 'energy' or how it releases it, for that matter. When Dad first picked this up, he nearly passed out, and his arm was numb for hours."

Buck cautiously picked it up, turning it around to inspect the back side. The back was flat, except for a depression about the size of a baseball. No other markings were visible. "So what is it?" He asked. "I can see it's made of some sort of crystal, but what is its purpose?"

"The texts we found call it a keystone. The outline is reminiscent of an obelisk, which is why we thought it might be Egyptian at first."

Buck could just see his hand through the crystal, and there was no evidence of anything but the crystal structure itself. Buck placed the obelisk back into the box.

Kate continued her explanation of the object. "The references we found were in an ancient Mesopotamian tablet that describes sets of keystones that could, if mishandled, actually kill a person. In fact, according to those texts, using these keys was necessary to gain access to a more powerful object. Something that was so powerful that only the wise could use the power in a constructive manner."

"That implies someone abused that power" Buck observed.

"Yes – You've heard of the Tower of Babel? Well, the tablet we have suggested the tower was built using this object – According to the text it was so large the height would have been awe-inspiring even today – and shortly after it was completed, a foolish priest misused this powerful object, called by several names; Mesopotamians called it by several names, such as the Tablet or Stone of Destiny. Later sources seem to be referring to a similar object called 'The Source' or the 'Power of God', but it was most often referred to as the 'Covenant Stone'.

"Anyway, this misuse of this Stone is apparently what caused the tower to collapse, killing thousands of people, and may have caused migrations away from the Mesopotamian basin to other lands. An earlier, less detailed text implies it was used by Noah in the construction of his Ark. There are a few other, even less detailed references to the stone, but that should give you an idea of how powerful this thing is supposed to be."

Jock replied "So what's the actual evidence of this Stone? It sounds like you can't really be sure about the validity of that story."

Kate said "That's simple – where there is a locked door, there is a key. And where someone takes the time to fashion a lock and key, especially one like this," Kate pointed to the obelisk-shaped crystal, "There is something very valuable. Even if the Tower story is just a myth or exaggeration of a real story, it is clear that someone believed it was necessary to lock up and protect this object from others. The archeological value alone could be worth a fortune."

Buck broke in "And at the very least, may be a way for surviving Nazi rats to finance a revival of their beloved 'Reich'. So I think I understand what these Germans are after, now tell me where you think we can help?"

Kate looked Buck in the eye. "Both of you fought in the war, and obviously have experience with people like this. You also spent time in the Middle East and North Africa, and most importantly, my father's friend - Who I trust - believes you are the right people to help me find Dad.

"And perhaps more importantly for you, I can pay you rather well for your services. I have a healthy inheritance from my mother's side of the family, so that will not be an obstacle where Dad's safety is concerned."

Buck said, "Listen Miss, you're asking us to pack up and head halfway around the world on what very well could be a wild goose chase. I'll admit I'm motivated by your story, but this won't be cheap. Besides our 'fees' and the cost of travel for Jock and myself, we need to cover for storage for our plane and gear that is staying here in Ecuador. This may cost you more than you realize."

Kate interrupted "Actually, Mr. Clark was pretty thorough when he told me about you. I know you own an amphibious aircraft with a small arsenal inside it. I suspect mobility will be important, so I think your plane is probably critical to our success. I intend to pay for passage for the two of you, your plane and gear, plus your 'fee'. "

Buck sat back and pushed his cap back on his head. He hadn't expected that. "So all travel costs to the Mediterranean and back - and $20,000 for our services."

Kate responded, "Yes – but I have two stipulations before I pay your price. First, I pay for your travel and transportation of your plane to and from the port of your choice in the Mediterranean, plus $5000 up front. The rest is payable *if* we find Dad and get him home alive. I have to keep you motivated, after all.

"Second, I will meet you in En Gedi, near where he was last seen. From there, I will accompany you until we find Dad."

"This could be ugly. Possibly violent, if Krause really is involved," Buck replied. He could tell she was determined to proceed. Even if she didn't know what she was heading into, she had already impressed him with her straightforward approach. Buck turned to Jock. "You Ok with taking the job?"

Jock nodded once, as Kate said, "Then I'll see you in Palestine. Two weeks from today".

Chapter 2 - En Gedi, Dead Sea - Palestine

A battleship grey JRF-6B Grumman Goose skimmed just above the surface of the Dead Sea. It was mid-morning and the bright blue sky provided a colorful contrast to the dusty brown hills of Palestine. Buck reached up and eased off the throttle, slowing the seaplane. The Goose gently eased into the salty inland sea, leaving a white, frothy wake behind. Buck steered the Goose towards their destination, a small dock at the water's edge.

A thick, white layer of salt encrusted the shores and the old wooden post supporting the dock, creating an eerie, other-worldly effect. Buck had never seen a place quite like it.

The settlement of En Gedi was not actually visible from the shore. It was set further back, up the hills to the west of the shoreline. En Gedi was a small village clustered around a natural oasis. As they approached from the air, Buck observed that there were no paved roads in or out, only old paths and trails, running parallel to the shoreline of the Dead Sea. As the paths stretched north, the hills on the west side of the sea steadily rose to form a rugged line of cliffs.

Now that the plane was approaching the dock, Buck recalled how his father insisted that he read the history of the Holy Land, and how that had eventually fueled an interest in ancient history. Buck recalled stories about the shepherd David, the future King of the Israelites hiding from King Saul in this area. It was indeed isolated, and the hills were supposedly littered with caves that could offer cover. Buck knew that his client's father had disappeared further north of here, after exploring similar caves in the more mountainous areas to the north.

Buck had to admire Kate's determination. This was not an easy place to reach by land.

They had parted ways with Kate Carter two weeks prior, with plans to rendezvous in En Gedi. True to her word, she arranged for a steamer transport from South America to Cadiz, Spain. Buck and Jock flew the Goose to Caracas by way of Bogota, where the plane was loaded onto the steamer Venture for the transatlantic trip. Once they docked in Cadiz, Spain, the Goose was unloaded and provisioned for their next leg, which was to follow the northern rim of the Mediterranean Sea.

The Goose gently eased into the salty inland sea

While in Cadiz, Kate had sent word that she would meet them in En Gedi. She would have ground transportation arranged to the site where her father found the obelisk-shaped keystone. From there, they hoped to retrace his path up until his disappearance – and hopefully find some clues to his whereabouts.

They left Cadiz and followed the major ports along the northern Mediterranean. Buck spent time on the ground in a few of those same cities, and was pleased to see some of the recovery after the war. Europe had not fully recovered yet, but he could already see some progress since he left a year earlier.

While they had been on the move nearly every day, Buck actually felt rested. He thrived on travel, so this was a welcome change. However, he knew it wouldn't last, and sensed that it was about time to earn their paycheck.

His thought turned to Kate and her father. At this point, Professor Emmitt Carter had been missing nearly a month, and Buck was not optimistic about finding him. Despite his misgivings, Buck had already decided that he liked Kate and wanted to try to help.

On the dock, a short, weathered old man was waving them down as the plane cruised closer. "That must be her contact, Oren," Buck called out to Jock "can you get the mooring line ready?"

"You got it boss. You see the lady yet?"

"Nope," Buck replied. "I know she's planning on meeting us with the transport – Hope its rugged enough for the trip up to the caves she mentioned. I expect that this guy we are meeting now will know exactly where she is."

As Jock stepped out onto the dock to tie her down, Buck went to collect their gear. A few minutes later, the Grumman was moored to the dock, while Buck carried a backpack out of the plane. The backpack was set on the dock, while Jock carried a bulky oblong leather-bound case. He wasn't in the habit of allowing their protection out of arm's reach.

They were approached by the small man. He was tanned and wrinkled, wearing equally wrinkled khaki shorts and shirt, topped off by a wide-brimmed straw hat. He extended an energetic hand to Buck and Jock. "Hello, I am Dr. Oren Shanks; allow me to welcome you to En Gedi. Miss Carter is expecting you. Please follow me."

After exchanging greetings, the two Americans shouldered their gear and followed Oren along the dock. "How do you know Miss Carter?" Buck asked.

Oren looked back with a wry smile, "To be honest, before this morning I only knew of her. However, I have known her father for years. We worked together on a few digs here in Palestine. He is a good friend, so I'll do whatever I can to help his daughter. "

"So you know why we're here", Jock said.

"Yes" the old man answered. "I hope you find Professor Carter soon. I am quite worried by his disappearance. I was concerned when he said he was investigating the caves north of here. They can be a dangerous place to visit."

"What do you think happened?" Buck asked. "Is there a chance he had some sort of accident in the caves?"

Oren replied, "Emmitt is experienced in the field. While I doubt he fell victim to an accident, that is possible. Emmitt is usually a very cautious man. What may be more worrisome is that I know he was onto something, so there may be more to this than we know."

The dock extended from a stony landing. The men followed a foot path leading to a sloping hill. The trio made their way up the long slope, following the Nahal Arugot stream. As the slope leveled out, their path approached a broad dirt road running parallel to the Dead Sea. Just to the far side of the road was a small mud-brick building with a small military style vehicle parked to one side. The oasis of En Gedi, with a handful of stone and brick homes, was another 400 yards further up the hill. Behind the settlement, the desert hills continued to climb above them.

Buck took his bearings and recalled his college years studying world history. He especially liked the maps of the ancient world. Over the Palestinian hills to the west were Gaza and the Mediterranean Sea; to the north and slightly west lies Jerusalem and Bethlehem; directly north would be Jericho. A short flight to the southwest was Cairo. Far to the east lies Iraq and Baghdad, and directly south were Sinai, Arabia and the Red Sea. They were in an ancient land.

As they approached the building with the transport vehicle, Buck recognized it as a Dodge three-quarter ton WC-51 four-wheel drive, with a canvas cover over the top for shade. It appeared to be a salvage vehicle from the war.

Jock caught Buck eyeing the old wartime transport. "Good choice for an off-road trip," he said. Buck nodded in agreement.

Oren indicated they should stow their gear in the back of the WC as Kate came out of the building.

"Hello boys," Kate said with a serious tone. "I hope you're ready to get going." She dropped a backpack onto the truck bed.

Kate turned to Oren, "Dr. Shanks, I can't say how much I appreciate your hospitality. I hate to leave so quickly, but we need to get to the caves as soon as possible. I think we have to move quickly"

Oren took her hand in both of his. "I wish you the best, and pray you find your father quickly. Please be safe."

"Dad left detailed notes on the caves he was interested in. We should be able to make it there and back today, assuming we find the site he was interested in."

"Take the time you need," Oren replied. He turned to Jock and Buck. "I will make sure your plane is well cared for while you are gone."

Buck thanked Oren for agreeing to care the Goose, as Jock asked Kate "Is the truck fueled and ready?"

"Yes" Kate answered, "I took care of that with the help of Mr. Shanks' sons this morning."

"Sounds good," Buck said. "Let's hit the road."

Jock took the driver seat as Kate sat next to him and pulled out a large map of the local area. She pointed out the trail they would follow parallel to the Dead Sea for the next hour or so.

Buck took a seat in the back and opened the large leather case Jock had been carrying. The case was packed with a sampling from their arsenal. The centerpiece was his father's 12-guage Browning shotgun, a double-hump Sears Ranger Repeater with a modified eighteen-inch barrel and the name 'Morty' carved into the butt of the stock. The collection included a .32 Winchester lever action rifle, 2 Colt .45 revolvers and a Webley Mk II .455 revolver. It also had bandoliers for carrying ammunition for the shotgun and the colts, holsters for each of the pistols, and a custom-made leather holster for carrying the shotgun across the back. Buck inspected each and took stock of ammunition, ensuring that the bandoliers were stocked. He looked up and saw

Kate staring at the collection of firearms. "Do you think we need those?" she asked.

"I hope not," Buck said, "but it's always better to hav'em and not need'em. The alternative isn't so great." He closed the box as they bounced along the trail. Kate eyed the weapons, and then slowly turned to face forward.

Buck felt a rush of sympathy for her. "How are you doing?" Buck asked in spite of himself. He always made a point to not get involved in his customer's emotional baggage, but this felt different.

Kate didn't turn around. She looked down at her lap and said "It's hard. But I have to believe we'll find him." She added after a slight pause, "Alive."

Buck put a hand on her shoulder. "We are going to do everything we can to find him," he replied. Buck then turned his attention their backpacks, and pulled out two bulky SCR -536 "handy talkie" self-contained radios, also called HTs. He performed a quick ops check, extending the antennas to activate them. Satisfied that both HTs were transmitting and receiving, he stowed one radio in a secure sling on the side of his backpack. Buck then checked to make sure they had filled canteens, rope, a smaller bag of pitons and carabiners for rock climbing, 3 rolled up sleeping bags, matches, two flashlights, several tins of food, packed with forks, a small knife and a can opener.

Satisfied that they had enough of the basics for a potential overnight stay, Buck separated the food and camping supplies into a box in the back of the truck. He then made sure the backpacks were set up with the climbing gear, one of the radios, flashlights and a canteen. The other radio would stay with the WC.

Buck turned his attention to the countryside, and pulled his Reds baseball hat down to shield his eyes from the glare. He watched the rugged hills to their left start to gradually grow larger, forming small mountains and cliffs to contrast against the flat blue glass of the Dead Sea to the right.

After an hour of driving, they drove over a dry creek bed spanned by a stone bridge. "That's the Nahal Kidron," Kate said. "Here is where we leave the main road." She then directed them to a small trail off to the left, winding up through a pass in the rocky hills. Buck noted the path was still passable but rough as they made its way up onto a ridge overlooking the Dead Sea. To the west, ahead of them, the ridge was topped with jagged cliffs.

The WC aggressively traversed the path about midway up the mountainside, crawling over the rocky terrain. They made their way along the base of a cliff towering at least a hundred yards above them before it became too steep to continue. Behind the WC the valley dropped nearly half a mile to the Dead Sea basin.

"Over there looks like decent cover" Buck said, pointing just to the left of the cliff base.

Jock pulled the WC into a hollowed area in the cliff base, out of site of the main road below. The tall cliff side provided welcome shade as they climbed out of the truck. "How close are we?" he asked as Kate pulled a leather-bound book out of her shoulder bag.

"We are close to the caves Dad was investigating. If I am reading this right, we are probably less than a half mile hike to the caves."

Buck took in their surroundings. To the east, the mountains sloped down to the Dead Sea Valley. On the north and south, cliffs stuck out like fingers towards the Sea. Between the cliffs, the ground rose steadily, but was too rocky and steep for the WC to climb. It was all barren, with no hint of vegetation or plant life. Near the end of the cliff to his right, several large natural buttresses extended from the extended end of the cliff, overlooking the valley below. The WC was parked at the base of one of these buttresses, partially blocking their view of the Dead Sea.

"What can you tell us about this area?" Buck asked. His interest in history was creeping to the surface, "Why would anyone hide artifacts like the crystal keys in this area?"

"Not a lot outside of Biblical tradition. We do know that after Rome destroyed Jerusalem in the first century AD, these hills offered shelter to many refugees, including temple priests. This area around the north half of the Dead Sea basin is riddled with caves that could hide thousands of refugees. The caves are so numerous, we don't even know of all of them.

"Some caves have even been enlarged into small complexes that were used to support people hiding from disaster or oppressors over extended periods. Most of that is tied to later periods, like the Roman oppression, but Dad and I think there was already a tradition of people either seeking seclusion or hiding valuables in this area. En Gedi was where David hid from Saul, for instance. Later religious officials would view this as an ideal place to either hide themselves or their treasures."

"Anyway, the Dead Sea was both a magnet and a source for early religious imagery. Some of the imagery we associate with the apocalypse or with hell actually comes from the Dead Sea. In fact, this area has some significance to ancient religions in general. Ancient Middle East tradition suggests this valley was a fertile, thriving area until God destroyed Sodom and Gomorrah. Both seem to be early settlements that thrived in this valley. After raining fire and brimstone down on those cities, the whole area was turned into a blasted, uninhabitable desolation.

"Fire and brimstone – essentially sulfur – is found nearly everywhere in this area, and the salt formations around the barren shoreline certainly contribute to the otherworldly appearance of this entire area. Since Sodom and Gomorrah were reputed to be in the Dead Sea basin, it's possible that the account of their destruction is based on some catastrophe that set off local sulfur deposits.

"In later tradition, Ezekiel prophesied that the Dead Sea valley will come back to life, with fresh waters that teem with fish. This rejuvenation of the valley would be a sign of the apocalypse. This could almost be viewed as a sign that evil would be banished from the world.

"The fact is that we don't know a lot about settlement or activity in this area. However, Dad stumbled upon a scroll that talked about glowing keystones that could unlock this power to the "Source" of Eden, or Covenant Stone if you prefer.

"What Dad found interesting is that like the Tower of Babel story, great destruction seems to be associated with an area that was either a possible location of the Covenant Stone or it's keystones, or has some relationship with Stone's lore. He was looking for a solid link between the Stone and the Sodom and Gomorrah story when he found the first obelisk keystone. The location of the second is what he was investigating when he disappeared. Of course, we don't know if anything is even still here, much less exactly where to look. The only lead I have are the caves described in his journal."

Kate scanned through the handwritten pages until she came to a sketch of the Dead Sea coastline. "We are probably pretty close to the cave Dad was interested in. Let me check our location against his notes."

Kate walked up to the ridge to get a view of the nearby coast. After looking over the hand-drawn map and the desolate valley below, she took out a compass and turned to face Buck and Jock. "I think we're close," she said. "We should be able to walk from here."

Buck approached her and asked "What are you using as a reference?"

'Do you doubt my ability to read a map?' Kate seemed to take offense at his question.

"No, not at all. I just want to know what we are using to get our bearings. "

Kate shrugged, and then pointed to the coastline. "You can see the dry bed of the Nahal Kidron, and the trail we followed up here. Those are the landmarks he shows in his notes. Dad also describes following a path upwards between steep cliffs that form near the top of the path; that matches our current location."

She turned to face the hills to the west, pointing up to the cliffs above them. "He then says to climb up towards two large vertical outcroppings of stone near where the two cliffs converge. I believe we can see them up there. At that point we follow the ridge back towards the sea until it ends in the buttressed formations overlooking the Dead Sea valley. We should find the entrance to his cave there."

Buck followed her hand, and saw two large upright fingers of stone about three quarters of a mile further up the rocky slope. It looked like a strenuous hike to that point, but not terribly difficult. Just to the right of the rocks, the path they needed to follow would be along the top of the cliff, back towards the Dead Sea. Buck estimated the top was a good 250 feet above their current location.

"Feel better now?" Kate asked with a slight smile. Buck found himself appreciating her all the more for being able to show a sense of humor despite her circumstances.

"Yeah, let's get going," he said. Turning to Jock, Buck called out "Jock, do you want to stay with the truck?"

"You got it Boss," Jock replied. He was already loading the Winchester. "I'll find some cover and make sure nothing sneaks up from this side."

Buck strapped on a belt with holsters and took the two colts. He offered Kate the Webley. "No," she said.

Buck grabbed his back pack, while Kate slung hers over her right shoulder.

"Suit yourself. I just want you to be cautious. We don't know what we will run into."

Jock settled into a small crevice near where Kate checked their location, where he could see the road below. He had the Winchester wrapped in old rags to hide any glint of metal in the sunlight and his HT was at his side, with antenna extended to switch it on. Jock signaled with a thumb up from his cover, as

Buck and Kate acknowledged and turned to start up the rocky slope.

As they climbed, Buck realized the old path up was steeper than it appeared from below, but still passable. Several times they had to climb on all fours. Kate didn't shy away from the dirty, rigorous climb. After some time, they reached the two upright stones. Buck looked at them. Something did not look right. "These aren't natural formations, are they?" he asked.

Kate looked at them. "They look like natural boulders, but they appear to have been placed here intentionally" she said. "They are just prominent enough to be seen from below, but I never considered them to be 'unnatural' in their placement until we got up close. These two rocks are too close in size and shape – and there are no other similar rocks nearby. You can see how they were 'planted' to stand upright on the flat surface of the ridge."

"So we are on the right track", Buck noted.

"I think so - we should go this way," Kate indicated it was time to bear to the right, following the flat crest of the ridge that extended over the shallow gorge below. As Buck looked around, he saw they were on one of several ridges that extended like fingers into the valley below. The ridge they were following was the most prominent.

Buck took out his canteen and offered a drink to Kate. "Was your father specific about which one of these ridges his cave is the right one? I assume we could find a network of caves in any of these cliffs."

Kate took a drink and handed the canteen back. "Only that he said it was to the southwest side of the ridges, and his journal implied it was on or around the ridge that had the clearest view of the Dead Sea valley. I think this one fits the description. But we could end up searching this entire area," She said with determination.

Buck nodded. "Ok. Let's do a quick check in with Jock before we go much further."

Buck dropped his backpack and pulled out his HT. He unscrewed the antenna cover and extended the thin metal rod underneath, activating the radio. Buck pressed the talk button and said, "Just checking in, Jock. How does it look on your end?"

"Clear for now," Jock's voice crackled over the HT. "Find anything yet?"

"No, we have to search the ridge. Kate thinks it should be close. I'll keep the talkie on as long as I can. If we head into a cave, I may need to stow it. I'll let you know before we do that, and check in as often as possible afterwards."

"Check. Watch your step up there. Jock out."

Buck stowed the HT with the antenna partly extended to keep it on, and shouldered his pack. "Ladies first," he said, with a slightly flippant attitude.

Kate rolled her eyes. "Such a gentleman."

"I've never been accused of that. Besides, I'd lead if I knew where we were going," Buck responded.

Kate pulled the leather book out again. She turned to the map she consulted earlier. "There's not a lot of detail drawn out here, but we seem to be in the right vicinity. Let's walk out to the end of this ridge and look for signs of a cave entrance."

After a few minutes, they reached the end of the ridge. At the end, the ridge spit into the natural buttresses they saw from below. Buck counted 4 buttresses. The top of each one sloped downward at a steep angle, then roughly 50 feet below, abruptly plunged straight down. In the distance, the still blue sea stretched out before them, separating Palestine from the hills and mountains of Transjordan to the East.

Buck suspected any usable caves were probably accessed from the sloped part of the cliffs. He could see how this area offered protection from invaders. "It may be hard to see any openings from up here. We may need to get down close to the edge to really see anything. Let me set up a rope as a safety line, and try to get a better view."

Buck walked over to the southernmost buttress, and studied the ground near the top edge of the slope. As Buck sat his backpack down, he saw they were directly above Jock and the WC.

Buck picked a suitable spot to sink a piton to serve as an anchor for the rope. He attached a carabiner to the piton loop and tied the rope to it, then placed another carabiner to his belt and looped the rope through it. Buck tied the rope into a Munter hitch to allow him to control the speed of descent.

Kate watched while Buck prepared his gear. Buck said, "This setup will work as a safety line for this sloped area directly below us. I'll go down first and look for the cave. If we need to go past the far cliff edge, we may need to do something a little more elaborate to stay safe. Once I've spotted the cave, I'll come back up and we can descend together." He handed her the HT. "Monitor this and yell if Jock calls, or if you see any trouble."

Kate took the radio. "Like what?"

Buck shrugged, "People with guns?" he replied as he carefully lowered himself down the rocky incline.

Buck worked his way down and to the south of his anchor point. He judged the slope to vary from forty-five to sixty degrees as he descended. His plan was to get just past the vertical drop off, then work from side to side to get the widest possible view of the cliff top. Once he was near the lower edge, caves or recesses that could not seen from above should be visible.

He worked his way across the lower cliff edge, moving to his right. Buck took his time, ensuring the safety line was secure as he alternated his focus from finding footing to scanning the ground in front and above him. Buck gradually worked his way across the cliff face, arcing around the outer edge of the drop-off. As he neared the north side of the buttress, he decided to look across his right shoulder towards the next one. He had assumed he would repeat the process of anchoring his rope and descending for each of the large stone outcroppings.

Directly to his right, in the crevice between the two buttress-like formations was a dark spot, a recess in the cliff wall. "Damn if that doesn't look like a cave entrance," Buck said out loud.

"You found it?" Kate yelled down.

"I found something – I need to get closer" Buck replied. He worked his way to within ten or fifteen feet of the darkened recess. Above the cave, between the top of the natural stone silos, Buck spotted very steep steps carved into the ground. He decided they looked very passable with a guide rope. The steps wound down to the left side of the entrance and ended in a small, flat landing in front of the cave. Buck realized one had to be close to see the steps. They were not likely to be spotted from above, and there was no way they could be seen from the base of the cliff.

Satisfied that he had found a likely candidate, Buck made his way back up to the crest of the ridge. Kate looked at him with raised eyebrows, so he explained "There is a cave, just between these two natural buttresses. There are some very old steps leading down to it, but I wouldn't recommend trying to hike down, at least not yet."

"Can we get to it?"

"Yes," Buck replied, "Let me move the guide line to just above the cave, and then we can probably get down without too much trouble."

Kate looked at the piton. "Yes, this looks like his. I've seen these in his gear." Buck could hear the hopefulness and the fear compete for control of her voice. "We have to be in the right place... We need to get down there, Mr. Haggard."

Buck agreed, and began by setting a new safety piton into the ground several feet back from the cliff edge. He tied the rope to it, and then set another piton at the top of the rocky slope. Buck knotted the rope around a carabiner, and clipped it to the second piton. As he put his backpack on, he said, "Let me go down and make sure I can set up a better guide rope for you. Once I'm done, I'll come back up and get you set up." Buck paused. "I can't have my client falling off a cliff now, when things are just starting to get interesting."

Buck worked his way down the steep slope, the rocky outcroppings extending to both sides. He could make out very old, worn-out steps as he went. Even when new, anyone

Directly to Buck's right was a recess in the cliff wall...

traversing this path would have to be sure-footed enough to make this ascent without a safety line. The path dropped away as the hillside became even steeper. Buck judged he was just about over the entrance. He spotted old foot and handholds carved into the rock. Buck could see a small ledge below, which should be in front of the cave.

Buck set another piton, and knotted the rope around a carabiner and hooked it. He used the rope to lower himself down the ancient steps to the ledge. Buck set another piton just inside the entrance and tied the rope off.

The cave entrance was about 6 feet high by 4 wide. Just inside the entrance, several stone steps led down to a dusty, flat floor. It had obviously been worked to be so flat. Buck's confidence in their location grew.

He stepped down into the cave and looked into the shadows. Buck couldn't yet make out much but could tell the cave went back quite a ways. He took his backpack off and set it on the floor. As he looked inside for his TL-122 flashlight, Buck caught movement out of the corner of his eye. Startled, he reached for his colt, and then realized Kate was standing in the entrance. She had made her way down without waiting.

"You were taking too damn long," she said.

Buck started to respond, then bit his tongue. 'Not worth it', he thought. Instead, he said "Let me see the radio."

He removed it from Kate's bag and called down to Jock. "Still clear from your position?"

Jock's voice crackled over the radio, "So far – Any luck up top?"

"We found a cave, it looks promising. About to go further in, so not sure how well the talkie will work. I'll leave it on near the entrance. If you see anything, holler and we should hear it. We'll try to check in every 15 minutes or so."

"Got it. I'll keep an ear open. Be careful up there."

Buck sat the HT, with antenna fully extended, just inside the cave entrance. He picked up the flashlight he had retrieved from his pack and switched it on. "What are we looking for in here?" he asked.

"On Dad's first trip, he said the cave had additional chambers carved off of the main cave." As Kate spoke, Buck swung the light around. He took note of the cave passage heading back away from the entrance. The floor looked as if had been worked, but the cave itself was clearly formed from natural erosion. As he directed the light to the back, he saw two rectangular doorways carved in the sandstone walls, both about five and half feet tall.

"Dad said that one of the chambers had what appeared to be a library, with a place to write or transcribe documents, and a few jars holding scrolls. In the other, was a series of niches, some sealed, some open. He found the keystone in that room, in a partially sealed niche. That room also appeared to have a tunnel excavated in it, but he didn't have time to explore it. He came back to look for more artifacts like the key, as well as check out the tunnel."

"Let's start in that one", Buck motioned to the door on their right. He shouldered his pack and ducked as he entered the chamber.

Inside was a circular room, carved out of the rock. On the walls were hundreds of small holes, or niches. Most were empty. Some were blocked with a plaster-like substance, and a few others showed evidence of plaster torn away. To the right side of the room, at floor level, a tunnel about four feet tall and wide fell away into the dark. Buck inspected the tunnel as Kate moved around the room looking at the man-made recesses in the walls. As he directed his light into the tunnel, he could see it was not entirely a natural formation. The floor had steps carved into it as it sloped down and away to the right. Buck recalled Kate's comments that the Dead Sea area had been a refuge during times of crisis 'I wonder if that's a back door' Buck thought to himself.

Kate had her light out and was examining one of the few niches that had been disturbed. "This one was recently opened. See how the dust isn't as thick, it's been brushed away. I think this is where the key was kept"

"What's carved above the niche?" Buck asked. Kate directed her lamp to the stone above the niche. Ancient pictographs were carved in the rock:

"Can you read it?" he asked.

"Yes" Kate replied. "It's a form of Paleo-Hebrew, and seems to be describing our current location. Paraphrased in English it says, 'Dead Sea Desert, north of Sodom'. Sodom's location isn't certain, but tradition holds it to be near the south end of the Dead Sea. One possible location is near En Gedi, which really isn't that far."

Kate paused a moment, considering the inscription, "I'm not sure of the purpose for it. Why describe where we are? Also, this script predates traditional Hebrew, so it suggests this cave may have been used as far back as around thirty-five hundred to four thousand years ago."

"Any clues to whether or not he made it back in here?"

"No, not that I can see. Let's look in the other room."

Buck led the way out and to the other doorway. As he swept his lantern around, he observed the second chamber was smaller, with several clay jars off to the left of the entrance. Most were intact, one had been broken. Rolled pieces of parchment were scattered in the debris. On the right was a large recessed area about 3 feet off of the floor and four feet wide. An ancient clay oil lamp and a handful of small pottery containers sat on it. Buck realized that it probably served as a desk or work table of sorts.

As he moved the light up the wall, something caught his eye. There were more carved letters in the wall above the "desk". One set matched the carvings in the other room:

Below that was another set of letters:

Then a strange line drawing etched below that:

Kate stepped in close to look at the carvings. The first inscription is the same as in the other room," she said. "The second…" Kate studied the glyphs, "the Feet of God." She turned her attention to the drawing. "Something doesn't look right here."

Buck looked closer at the drawing. The lines had a different consistency, as if drawn by a different hand, and at a different time. He put the light up close. He realized that new, clean stone was visible in the etched lines.

"Is that a recent addition?" he asked. Then, "Do you think your father did that?"

"I don't know," Kate said. "What would be the purpose?"

"A message perhaps…. He came here searching for a second keystone – or at least clues to its location, right?"

Kate nodded, and Buck continued, "And now we know he disappeared after this point in his trip. I think, based on what you've told me, that he knew someone was either following him or he was in some sort of danger. And, he left his notes with you."

Buck looked at Kate. "I think he expected you to come looking, and this is meant for you. Your father knew you would figure it out."

Kate looked at the carvings. "The first inscription is our current location" she said. "And both rooms have some sort of message transcribed…" Kate thought a moment. "The niche! I wonder if that's where he found the keystone I have." She took out her father's journal, found a blank page and began sketching the carvings. "This may be important. I need to make a copy."

Buck swept his light across the room again. "This room looks like a place where documents where kept – or at least transcribed… What if the 'transcriber' was also leaving a message – indicating locations for something – Is it possible the phrase 'Feet of God' is somehow tied to a location?"

Kate's attention did not waver from the carvings. "You may be right," she said. "I think I see it now. He's telling us –"

Just then the radio near the cave entrance crackled to life "Buck! Get a move on, we have company!"

Buck raced to exterior chamber, grabbed the HT and pressed the transmit button. "What do you see, Jock?"

"Two trucks, look like war surplus, loaded with men. I could just make out rifles with my binoculars. They drove past, but slowed as if looking for something."

"Are you sure they aren't some locals?"

"No. Big blond guy driving and everyone I could see looked pretty white. And armed to the teeth - My guess is it's the krauts." Jock replied.

"Heading out," Buck responded. He looked over at Kate. She had entered the outer chamber and was putting her journal away. "We need to go. Now," He said.

They were prepared to head out of the cave as Jock called again, "Buck! They just went off road about a half mile north. I lost visual as they headed west into the cliffs. I'm concerned they are circling back towards you from above the ridge."

"Check," Buck responded. "Kate, stay here a minute, I need to recon the path up. Sit tight."

Buck stepped out onto the rock ledge, and began climbing the nearly vertical steps. As he neared the top he kept close to the ground. Just over the top lip of the slope, he looked for telltale signs of vehicles. Buck spotted a plume of dust to the northwest. It appeared to be moving in his direction. 'No time to pull the pitons and ropes' he thought. That would almost immediately give his position away.

Buck backed down the staircase, weighing his options. There weren't many. As he entered the cave, Kate said, "Let me guess. People with guns?"

Buck replied, "Lots, based on what Jock said. And this is not the time or place for a stand."

"We're cornered," Kate said. "What choice do we have?"

"The tunnel in the first chamber heads down. Come with me."

Kate shook her head. "You have to be kidding. We don't know where that goes."

Buck looked her in the eye. "It's either a back door, or it goes down and opens to more chambers. If we are lucky, it'll lead to an exit. Worst case, we're still cornered and have to fight anyway. In either case, it's a bottleneck that we can defend, which gives us a greater chance than an all-out firefight."

"What makes you think there will be a way out?" she asked, still unsure of his plan.

Buck grabbed Kate's wrist and pulled her behind him into the back room. "We're wasting time. I'm all ears if you have a better plan," he said. As they entered the narrow tunnel, Buck handed her a light. "Take this and lead the way, I'll keep an eye out for our guests."

Kate grudgingly took the light, and started down the tunnel. As they turned the corner she whispered, "You had better be right. If we get caught…"

Buck put his index finger up, signaling to be quiet. There were sounds of movement in the outer chamber. He heard a gruff voice "Suche das Mädchen!"

Kate looked at Buck with a question in her eyes. He softly whispered "They're looking for you." Buck motioned her to move on.

Kate led the way down the tunnel. Buck continued to listen for sounds that might indicate people following them, but heard nothing yet.

The tunnel continued to curve to the right, almost in a spiral downward. Buck was unsure of their direction as the passageway levelled off and headed straight ahead. 'We seem to be deeper into the mountainside' he thought. After about a hundred yards, the tunnel took a hard right turn. As they rounded the corner, the floor seemed to disappear from under their feet. Buck and Kate fell into pitch blackness; they found themselves sliding down a sandy incline. After what seemed like an eternity, Buck felt his behind hit level ground. Just Buck realized they had stopped, Kate landed on top of him.

Buck took his light and pointed it up the slope. It was a near 45 degree slope upwards into darkness.

"Well that was fun," he quipped. "You OK?"

Kate stood up and knocked the dirt off. "Yes. A few bumps but no injuries that I can tell." She looked around for her flashlight. Picking it up, she inspected their surroundings. It appears to be a natural cave, just over 8 feet high and about twenty five feet long. She could see no visible openings to the outside. "What now?"

"We find the way out," Buck replied.

Kate raised her eyebrows, "Please explain your reasoning," she said. The doubt in her voice was obvious.

Buck looked around as he said, "I think this passage is a way in or out – probably an exit in case of invasion. That incline is man-made, and it's designed to go one way – down and my guess is out." He started to walk towards the opposite end of the cave. "If the caves in this area were used to hide from invaders, it only makes sense there would be emergency exits."

Buck stopped near the end of the cave and looked at the wall. "I realize that's a calculated risk," he said as he switched his light off. "Shut your light off."

Kate complied, and realized she could still see. A narrow beam of light was filtering in from the top of the wall. "There is a way out. Well, Mr. Haggard, I'm impressed."

"Me too," Buck said with a grin. He started pulling rocks and dirt away from the light. Soon the narrow hole was large enough to crawl through. Kate was about to climb through when Buck stopped her.

He unshouldered his backpack, and indicated Kate should do the same.

"Wait here - I'll go first and look for a suitable place for us to hide. I'm not sure where we are coming out, so we need to look for cover as soon as we get out. Remember our guests are on top of the ridge, and if they see us we are sitting ducks."

"When I come back, give me the bags then I'll pull you through. Be ready to move fast."

Buck climbed up through the hole and into the sunlight. The glare in his eyes made it hard to see. After a few seconds, he realized they were up against the cliff base, at the top of the slope facing the Dead Sea. Buck scanned the area for familiar landmarks. Off about a mile to his right and in the valley below was the road they came up earlier in the day. He judged that Jock and the WC were probably just around the base of the cliff, less than a quarter mile away.

Buck looked up. There was a slight overhang above the cave exit, so getting out should be easy. It was the quarter mile trek to Jock that had Buck worried.

Buck reached down into the cave, and signaled for Kate. She handed him her bag and his backpack, then grabbed his hand. Buck pulled her up and out. They grabbed their gear and Buck led the way around the cliff base. As they rounded a buttress-like formation Buck looked up. He could barely see the ledge that served as the front doorstep to the cave above. Here is where they were in plain view if someone were to look down. "There is no way that a lookout hasn't been posted up there", Buck whispered. "We take our chances and run around the cliff base for Jock and the WC, OK?"

"OK," Kate agreed.

"Now!" Buck grabbed Kate's arm and took off. Up above, Buck heard someone call out "Aussehen! Ich sehe sie unten! <Look! I see them down below!>"

Bullets struck the ground near Buck and Kate as they rounded the cliff base. Jock was waving from his hiding place between several large boulders. He jumped into the WC and started it.

Two dark figures appeared on top of the cliff as they piled into the WC. Shots were fired from above as Jock readily handled the large truck over the rough terrain. Buck pushed Kate down into the floorboard. "Hey!" she exclaimed. Buck ignored her and drew his colt, firing up towards the men on the ridge.

"Keep covering - We'll be well on our way before they get down to the road," Jock said.

"Let's not waste any time getting back to En Gedi anyway," Buck replied. "They won't be all that far behind."

As they took the main road heading south, Kate climbed up into the passenger seat. Buck kept an eye on the road behind them. Jock asked Kate "Did you find anything?"

"Yes. A clue, anyway."

Buck said "Back in the cave, you said you thought you had something. What was it?"

"I know where Dad was headed next. It hit me while looking at the carvings, that I've seen that before."

"The two towers?" Buck asked.

"They aren't towers," Kate said. "Not exactly. They are obelisk-shaped stones, and they are in a special place. That's where we have to go next."

Jock and Buck looked at Kate.

"We have to fly to Wadi Musa," she said. "To the lost city of Petra."

Chapter 3 - Wadi Musa, Shara Mountain Range - Transjordan

The Shara Mountain Range rose in front of three horse-mounted travelers like a rugged, red-tinted wall of stone. Buck, Kate and a local hired guide were outfitted with supplies for a short and potentially troublesome trip into the mountains. Buck had his 12-guage Ranger strapped across his back with one of his bandoliers, and Kate had accepted Buck's Webley revolver holstered to her right leg. On the back of her saddle was a small backpack with the Keystone safely bundled inside. The Arab guide, Ghaleb, had an old British EnfieldP-13 strapped to his horses' side for protection. He took the lead as they worked their way up the hillside out of Wadi Musa.

As the three riders made their way towards the red mountain range to the west, Buck reflected on the events of the previous afternoon.

Buck, Jock and Kate had landed at a small private airfield on the far side of the town of Wadi Musa. They had just enough time in the evening to find the Wadi Musa souq, or marketplace, to locate a guide and obtain lodging for the night. The souq is the open-air market common in many towns and cities throughout the Middle East. Buck observed that entering one of these souqs was almost like stepping back in time. Even in his wartime days in Cairo, when browsing the markets, Buck felt he was stepping through a doorway into an older way of life.

Most shops were wood-frame structures with woven tapestries or blankets draped over the top and two or three sides providing shade and a little privacy to do business. They were placed so close as to almost be on top of one another, which gave the impression of a chaotic and dynamic atmosphere. Bartering for all manner of goods was going on all around. An incredible variety of goods were for sale; food, drink, clothing, spices, woolen and silk carpets along with a vast array of other goods were for sale, and all of it was locally grown or made.

The late afternoon air was alive with the sounds of merchants vying for attention or bartering with customers. The art of negotiation was in full display here, as buyers and sellers worked each other to get the best deal possible.

As they passed through the crowded streets, merchants attempted to draw them into the small, open-air shops hoping to make a sale. Buck led the way as they navigated the market, occasionally stopping to inspect food goods, or avoiding the occasional spice merchant or Arab trader pulling a camel through the crowd.

Buck was able to locate and line up a local Bedouin guide named Ghaleb while Kate and Jock found lodging. The last order of business for the day was to get some food.

Over dinner at a local restaurant, Buck decided to regroup on the day's events. The three travelers ordered a platter of Mensaf, or lamb cooked in dried yogurt, falafel and flat bread with mezze sauce for dipping. As they waited for the food, Buck started by asking Kate to explain why she believed her father came to Wadi Musa and Petra.

"After you pointed out the drawing with the inscriptions was probably a message for me, I realized I had seen that picture before. If you recall, the first inscription was a description of where we were, and it was right above a carved niche. One intended to hold an object less than 12 inches tall."

"You mean the keystone?" Jock asked.

"Yes. And in the second room, we saw 2 inscriptions – the first one described the same location, 'Dead Sea Desert, north of Sodom'. The second inscription was another location description, but I didn't realize it until I thought about the drawing. The writing reads 'The Feet of God'. I assumed it was a reference to God as a deity, but it's more than that."

Buck thought about it, and asked, "The drawing – it's connected to that, right?"

"Right, the Feet of God is also an obscure reference to an ancient monument hidden on a mountaintop in this area. I believe the drawing is actually a sketch of it. Dad brought me here as a girl, and I've seen it. It took me a minute to make the connection between the inscription and Petra. This monument is located on a mountain within the Hidden Valley of Petra, and is part of an ancient worship complex called the High Place of Sacrifice."

Buck thought out loud, "And coincidentally, based on the cave drawing, this monument looks like a pair of obelisks. Does that suggest a connection to your obelisk-shaped keystones?"

"That may be a distinct possibility," Kate replied. She went on to explain that Petra was known as an ancient settlement by a group of people called the Nabateans, who used the location to control trade routes between North African and Mesopotamian peoples. It was also known by much older names such as Raqmu, Rekem and Sela. The majority of the visible or obvious settlements date from 4th century BC to the late 1st century AD when it fell to the Romans, but the valley had been in use thousands of years prior to that. The Nabateans exposure to different cultures had probably played some influence on the architecture that survived in the valley.

"So it's like a lost city hidden in the mountains?" Jock asked.

"Somewhat, yes," Kate said. "It's often referred to as the 'Lost City', although I think that is a little over-used. Petra was occupied by Crusaders for a short time, and after the crusades ended, it became 'lost' to westerners for several hundred years. At any rate, it's an incredibly impressive place to see."

Kate went on to explain that in 1812, Swiss explorer Johann Ludwig Burckhardt deceived some local Bedouin tribes and entered the hidden valley disguised as an Arab trader. He didn't take long to relate his discovery to the western world. Since then it has been considered an archeological marvel, but access was still limited. Political instability slowed western access to Petra, and for those that did make it to Wadi Musa, a local guide was usually necessary to ensure safe passage.

After dinner, they made their way to the local inn. Sleep came fast, and the next morning found the travelers ready to get started. Over breakfast, Jock volunteered to stay with the plane and ensure they would be ready to takeoff while Buck and Kate ventured into the Shara Mountains.

Buck's thoughts returned to the present as the town of Wadi Musa fell away behind them. Ahead, the dusty path ahead became a wide, shallow depression between the rising foothills of the Shara Mountains. A quarter mile further up, the path veered to the right behind the rocky hills.

Their guide motioned to either side, drawing Buck's attention to structures on either side of the path. On both left and right sides were shapes carved into rocky outcroppings, some displaying a strange geometric architecture. One façade on his left had four obelisk-shaped towers over a set of openings into the rock. Doorways within the façades revealed dark openings. Buck could not tell if the chambers inside were man-made or natural caves that had been artificially altered.

Kate took notice of Buck's interest in the carved structures. "I take it you're impressed by the carvings?" she asked.

"Very much so," Buck admitted. "What more can you tell me about this place?"

"First of all, don't get too excited– You haven't seen anything yet," she said with a smile. "These carvings barely compare to what you are about to see."

Their guide slowed his horse down and fell between Buck and Kate. He spoke in heavily accented, but well-practiced English. "Our town takes its name from the valley. Wadi Musa is named for the prophet you Americans call Moses. Here is where many believe he struck a rock and found water for his tribes. Many say that he dwelt here during the years in the wilderness."

Buck asked Ghaleb "What do you believe – Is that true?"

Ghaleb though for a moment, "I believe the prophet Musa was here. Near here is where his brother, the Prophet Haroun, that you call Aaron, is buried. On the far side of the Hidden Valley is Jebel Al-Haroun, where you can find his tomb. I believe we are near Holy Ground."

He paused, "Your business here is your own, but I hope you respect where we are."

"We do," Kate said. "And please understand that we are only here to search for clues to my father's location. We think he came here several weeks ago, before he disappeared."

"Then may Allah guide you," Ghaleb said. "We are near the Siq. I will need to speak with my B'doul clansman to enter the valley."

Buck was quiet as they followed the path to the right. Ahead the path widened to a flat area with a dry stream bed, or wadi, to the left, with reddish-brown cliff walls rising behind that. There was a rough stone bridge crossing the wadi. The path appeared to veer off to the left behind a turn in the cliff wall. On the far side of the dry waterway, nestled below the cliff wall was a Bedouin tent. A small brown-skinned Arab sat in front of a campfire. The three riders approached until Ghaleb signaled them to stop and wait. All three dismounted, and Ghaleb led his horse by the reigns, approached the man. He offered a greeting in Arabic. They spoke for a few minutes, both gesturing towards Buck and Kate at different times. A few minutes later, Ghaleb walked back. Addressing Kate, he said "Was your father's name Emmitt Carter?"

Kate looked up, "Yes. Was he here?"

"He did come here. We gave him permission to enter the valley, but did not return. After a few days, my friend went to look for him, but found only an empty tent at the base of Jebel Al-Mahdbah. We do not know what happened to him."

Kate looked at Buck, who said, "At least that confirms we're on the right path."

"There is more to be aware of. Other white men have been entering the valley. They do not seek help or guidance from us.

Their secrecy betrays who they are... I believe they are probably involved in your father's disappearance."

Ghaleb turned to address Buck. "I know from our talk you want to go to the mountain Jebel Al-Mahdbah, which is also where your father was last seen. I can take you into the valley, to the foot of the mountain. If you must go up to the High Place, the trail starts where I will take you, but from there you are on your own. I will wait for you at the bottom."

Buck nodded, "Yes and thank you for the hospitality. I think you may be right about these men. We have already had one close call with them in Palestine. If there is trouble, don't stick around - We can handle ourselves and we don't want to put you in unnecessary danger. We really just need someone to point us in the right direction."

Ghaleb replied, "It is not far. Let us go now." He turned and mounted his horse.

Buck and Kate followed suit, and the three riders set off on the trail. As it took a left turn the path seemed to intersect with the cliff walls in front of them. The path narrowed ahead, with 40 to 50-foot cliff walls closing around them. Buck noticed traces of worked stone, carved out of the sandstone walls. The remains of an arch that had once spanned the gorge ahead stood on either side of the path. The walls on either side of the arch had large niches carved directly into the natural stone. The floor of the gorge sloped downward, while the cliffs grew taller and the path narrowed ahead.

Kate continued her exposition on the local area, "This is called the Siq. It's the only direct entrance to the hidden valley. I remember this as a girl. It seemed to go on forever, but in reality is only about a mile long. The inhabitants here were master craftsmen, and you can see the traces of water courses, essentially freshwater channels they cut into the rock to supply the valley. There are also carvings along these walls, but many are so old and weathered they can be hard to see."

Buck looked up. He tried to imagine what it would have been like for a traveler walking to riding into this valley thousands of years ago. Faded relief carvings were just discernable in some areas.

As they passed a small shrine carved into a stone in the middle of the path, Kate spoke up, "Ghaleb is right about connections to Moses and Aaron. There is a rich tradition here that suggests those patriarchs did spend time here. In fact, the mountain we are about to climb may be far more significant to Biblical history than most realize."

Jock walked across the airfield to a hanger near where the Goose was parked. He had just arranged for enough fuel to fill the Goose's tanks. The airfield manager directed Jock to speak to Abdullah, his mechanic. He could be found in the old hangar to the west side of the runway. He hoped the mechanic's English was better than the manager. Jock was fluent in Spanish and French, but that was of no use here in Jordan.

Jock approached the hangar, and saw a Bedouin-style camp with cots and rugs to sit on to one side of the building. A small fleet of old fuel and maintenance trucks were parked behind the camp.

The hangar doors were open with a fuel truck was parked inside. A young boy was stowing a large fuel hose in the back.

Jock found Abdullah in a cluttered room in the back of the hangar, reading a magazine. He was dressed in dirty white coveralls, with his back to the door. When Jock knocked on the door to get his attention, the mechanic quickly stuffed the magazine under some papers scattered on his desk, but not before Jock caught a glimpse of the centerfold. "Was that Miss January?" he asked with a smirk.

Slightly embarrassed, the Abdullah ignored his question. "You must be the American we are refueling this morning," Abdullah said. "We will have the truck over to your plane shortly." His English was impeccable.

Jock responded, "Thanks. Before you start, is American cash acceptable for payment? If not, I may need to go into town to try to exchange for local currency."

Abdullah shook his head, smiling. "No need to do that, my friend. I accept all major currencies."

Jock reached for his pocket as the Arab gestured for him to wait. "We can settle up afterwards. Please make yourself comfortable as you wait," The Arab mechanic said. "I have some good magazines to read if you are interested."

Jock declined, and soon found himself walking around the small camp. A large, broad-shouldered man was now sitting on the rugs, tending a small fire and smoking a cigar. He was wearing brown pants, military-style riding boots and a khaki shirt. He had short dark hair and needed a shave. Jock thought he looked like Eurasian stock, probably southern Russian or Georgian descent. Jock thought, 'This guy looks about as out of place here as I do.' The stranger gave Jock a slight nod, acknowledging his presence. Jock returned the nod silently, and walked behind the camp, towards the trucks he observed earlier.

As he wandered between the old flight line equipment, Jock found himself between a fuel hauler to his right, and an old Mercedes cargo truck to his left, Jock glimpsed a sudden movement out of the corner of his eye. He spun around on instinct, but was too late. A dull thud and sharp pain shot through his head and the ground rushed up at him. Jock went black.

Buck and Kate rode slowly through the Siq, the narrow cliff walls blocking the mid-morning sun. Buck looked up, amazed at this natural hallway that must be hundreds of feet tall. He thought he could see a bright but uneven vertical sliver of light ahead. 'Must be near the end of this passage', Buck thought. The light grew brighter, but there was clearly another wall beyond the exit ahead. He could tell it was reddish in color like the rest of this canyon, but something did not look right. His eyes were still adjusting from the shadows of the Siq.

Ghaleb turned around and smiled, "You are about the see a most beautiful thing, Habibis. Behold the Al-Khazneh!"

The Siq's close walls fell away and opened into a wider canyon that ran to the right and left of the travelers. About a hundred yards to the left, the canyon dead-ended. To the right, it continued in a northwestern direction. Directly opposite the exit from the Siq, carved into the sheer rock face of the canyon wall was the most staggering sight Buck had ever seen.

A 140-foot, two-story façade reminiscent of Greco-Roman architecture towered over them. Etched from living rock, this had not been built, but beautifully and artfully carved. On the first floor, a massive door, more than twenty feet high, opened into dark rooms inside the structure. Columns framed the door as if they had grown in place. Ornate carvings on the top story sat between more columns. In the center was a recessed area, containing a rounded structure with columns, topped off with a conical roof. At the very top was a sort of decorative urn.

Kate broke the silence, "It's really something, isn't it?' she quietly said.

Buck agreed. He slowly started to take in his surroundings, and became aware that this overwhelming site was not the only structure carved into the cliff walls, although the Al-Khazneh was certainly the most impressive and elaborate. Columns, facades, geometric shapes all carved from the existing stone.

Nothing was placed, it was shaped from the environment. Buck scanned the walls to either side and behind him. "Incredible."

Kate replied, obviously in her element. "This was all done by the Nabateans, mostly around the time of Christ. Probably a bit before that by a couple of centuries, but we aren't 100 percent sure of the dates yet.

"Most of these are actually tombs - burial chambers for wealthy Nabateans," Kate continued. "They carved very elaborate tombs and shelters into the cliff walls within the valley. These ruins are at least as impressive as ancient Rome or the Pyramids, but there is more to the valley than just the carved rock tombs.

There is evidence of habitation going back at least 7000 years, and as you heard from Ghaleb, Petra may be a key location for some events in the Old Testament.

"The Nabateans controlled the nearby trading routes between Egypt, Syria and Persia. All of these carvings, including the ones we saw outside the valley, are Nabatean artifacts. In fact, a major route out of Egypt to the north is just outside of town, we saw it flying in. That was known as the King's highway and was a primary source of their wealth.

"In fact, there is some evidence that supports Ghaleb's belief that Moses stayed here along with the Israelites. I do think this valley has a much longer history than the Nabatean culture, and may be a prominent locale from the Old Testament. But most scholars don't recognize this, at least not yet."

"I'm intrigued," Buck said, as Ghaleb led them down and to the left, deeper into the rose-red canyon. "But in all honesty, I've been intrigued since we started here this morning. I have always liked biblical-era history, so I would love to hear more, if you don't mind."

Kate flashed a rare smile. "Of course. As our guide said, there is a long-standing tradition that Moses was here. As you know, the local town and this valley both carry the name Wadi Musa. The common belief is that this is where Moses drew water from the stone. That is probably linked to the abundance of small wells and man-made water courses that kept this valley fertile in ancient times. I don't know how accurate that belief is, but there are other reasons to believe Moses may have come through here.

"First, consider the route Moses would have taken out of Egypt. The Bible tells us he did not come the "way of the Philistines", which means along the Mediterranean coast. It was too well controlled by Egypt. The southern route, which most people seem to believe in, goes around the southern Sinai Peninsula, which makes no sense. The goal would have been to get away from Egypt as quickly as possible. Southern Sinai had Egyptian mines, and simply would have taken too long if it were a clear road. It also implies a Red Sea crossing at its widest point."

Behold the Al-Khazneh!

Kate looked sideways at Buck and smirked, "And don't get me started on the matter of the Red Sea..."

"You don't believe it happened?" Buck asked.

"Oh, it did – just not the way we modern, supposedly civilized people have interpreted it. Let's come back to that later, it is a subject all by itself."

"By all means, Professor, I would appreciate the education. I actually find ancient history fascinating. Believe it or not, I studied ancient world and medieval European history as part of my graduate work joining the OSS." Buck paused, "I was going to teach history, but then the war started."

Kate did a near double-take. "Graduate work? And to be a teacher? You are full of surprises, Mr. Haggard."

Buck shrugged it off, not really wanting to talk about it. "So what about the Exodus route? I recall from Sunday school that Moses went south, so if not the southern route around the Sinai Peninsula, what does that mean?"

Kate was immediately absorbed back into the conversation. "First of all, 'South' is relative to where the Exodus started, which was in Goshen, or northern Egypt. Next, think about where he was going, and why." She started ticking off her fingers as she spoke. "His goal was to get out of Egypt fast. He was going to Midian, which is historically the north part of the Arabian Peninsula, next to the Negev desert; in other words, right next door to this place. There was a major trade route going through middle Sinai, which leads right up to Midian's doorstep."

Buck saw the connection. "The King's Highway, just outside of town. That makes sense."

Kate continued, "On the subject of Midian, remember that is where he has his encounter with God — So Mount Sinai, or Mount Horeb, whichever name you subscribe to, along with the burning bush had to be in or near Midian. Placing the mountain of God in Sinai doesn't really make sense, geographically, at least not based on those facts. Moses was heading straight through the Sinai wilderness to freedom, and there were existing trade routes that make that a viable passage." Kate took a breath. "My father and I believe the King's Highway, which comes from Egypt and leads up north past the Dead Sea and towards Syria, was very likely part of the Exodus route, and why we think the Israelites came through here."

Buck thought for a moment, then said, "OK, I'll buy the Israelites came near here, and maybe even camped here. This canyon affords a lot of natural protection. Aside from that, what makes it so special, though? You seemed to imply this place was of some significance to the Exodus story. Or did I read too much into your earlier comments?"

"You didn't assume too much, Buck" Kate said. "But I think I would rather show you than just tell you."

Buck, Kate and Ghaleb rode silently through the canyon. Carved facades and reliefs etched into the sheer walls all around them. As they rounded a curve, the wall to the left fell back, revealing that it was the base of a small mountain, and the small canyon widened into a valley. Far ahead, to the north, the ground along the cliff walls formed a ramp that elevated into a large platform with even more elaborate buildings etched into the stone walls above it. Carved doorways and columns were visible in the base, level with the canyon floor.

Just ahead, at the foot of the mountain, was a huge roman-style amphitheater carved into the rock. Between the amphitheater and the large platform, the canyon floor fell away to more carved structures in the distance.

On the far side of the amphitheater, the canyon split into a larger north-south valley. The valley opened up to south, rounding the spur of the mountain that formed the left wall of the canyon they had just passed through. Across the valley, the far mountainsides were also dotted with elaborately carved doorways.

Ghaleb broke his silence. "Here is where I wait, Habibis. I will not set foot on this mountain today." He turned to Buck. "Please make sure you look ahead as you come back down. If I am not here tending our horses, be careful."

Ghaleb pointed to a rocky spur, jutting out from the foot of a mountain behind them. The spur was shaped into a platform about eight feet high. Large, knee-high steps provided a way up from the ground. On the back of the platform an ancient, rough-hewn set of steps ascended the mountainside, winding up and out of site around the rugged mountain clefts.

Ghaleb said, "Start here. The path is clear, and easy to follow. Still, be careful – there are sudden turns and it is steep. A fall will be the end of you."

Buck and Kate dismounted, and Buck handed the reins of both horses to the guide. "Thank you for your help and hospitality. We will try to get back as soon as possible." Buck took his gear from the horse as he spoke. Kate shouldered her backpack and checked her holster to make sure it was secure. Buck removed his shotgun and checked to make sure all six slugs were loaded. He placed it into the holster across his back and adjusted the bandolier, which was loaded with extra 12-guage cartridges. "We'll be as careful as possible," he said with a smile.

Jock awoke with a splitting headache. As his eyes slowly adjusted, he saw he was in a small, dimly lit chamber. Jock's hands were tied behind his back, and he had a gag in his mouth.

The floor beneath him was wood, but he was propped up with his back against metal. Canvas walls were on either side. 'I'm in one of the cargo trucks' he thought. He didn't sense any movement, so he assumed he was still at or near the air field.

He thought back, trying to recall any clues that might tell him who had attacked him. There was no question in his mind that the Germans from Palestine were behind this. Jock thought about the morning events leading up to this. The stranger at the camp had to be involved.

Jock tested his restraints. His feet were tied together with half inch rope. His hands were tied behind his back, presumably with the same. He could tell his hands and feet were connected by the rope, so he could not fully straighten out or stand up. The gag was tight enough to keep him from making loud sounds, but did not restrict his breathing.

As Jock looked around, he scanned the truck bed for anything that could be used to cut or fray the rope. No luck. Jock heard someone approaching from the outside. The canvas flap at the rear of the truck parted. Jock squinted as light flooded in, then a hulking shadow blocked the light.

A large man stepped up into the truck. The man had his back to Jock as he closed the canvas flap. In his left hand was a German army-issued C96 Mauser pistol. As he turned around, Jock's eyes shifted from the gun to the man's face. Jock recognized him almost immediately.

Wilhelm Krause smiled at Jock. An evil, relentless smile. Krause stepped towards Jock and pulled the gag off. He kept the Mauser pointed at Jock. "We meet again, Lieutenant Howard. You slipped away from us in Palestine. Quite lucky, I must say. I trust Captain Haggard is not far away?" Krause's accent was underscored by the venom in his voice.

Jock quietly looked Krause in the eye. Krause took the silence as his answer. "I suppose he is. You two are never that far apart. Where did he go this morning?" Jock glared, refusing to answer.

"If he went to the Ruins in the Red Valley, I think we will find him soon enough." Krause holstered his gun. "And if we don't find him there, he will still make his way back here – and then we can have a bit of fun, no?"

The two Americans made their way up the ancient steps, passing partially eroded tombs and facades to their left. The mountain dropped away on the right as they worked their way up the winding stone path.

Buck took the lead as Kate asked, "How much of the Bible have you read, Mr. Haggard? In particular, Moses' journey from Egypt, and how the Israelites came to take part in the covenant on Mt Sinai?"

Buck looked back. "I assume this has some relevance to where we are. I don't recall a lot of the detail, just the general Exodus story and that Moses received the commandments on Sinai. I also remember that is where he first saw the Burning Bush and encountered God. I'm not sure I see the connection here, because that was supposed to have happened in the Sinai Peninsula – that's pretty far away from here."

"The origin of the name Sinai is not fully understood, and the exact location is actually very unclear, partly because the Bible translations we have are copies of earlier copies. The original text – the first edition, if I can say it that way – has never been found. We don't really know what redactions or alterations may have occurred, even inadvertently. There is evidence that the original story is extremely old. The bottom line with place names is that they tend to be fluid, and perhaps indicate general regions more than being very specific or a town or landmark. That means we have to rely on tradition to some degree.

"If you think about Moses' flight from Egypt as a young man, he went to Midian. Midian is considered to be in the modern Arabian Peninsula. Midianites did frequent western and northern Arabia, and we are on the northern border of that region."

As they followed the path it occasionally changed from steep, cut stone steps to sandy, nearly flat stretches. The flat areas afforded some relief from the ascent, but always led to more steep climbing. It was clear from the construction and placement of the stepped areas that this had been an important path. Some areas required a strenuous hike, but nothing was impassable or too difficult. The two adventurers made steady progress up the mountainside.

Kate continued, "As I said earlier, the idea that Moses met Midianites in the southern Sinai peninsula is not that plausible or even logical. It was too close to Egypt, who also had mining interests in that region. It's far more likely he fled straight East to Midianite territory, where his new family was. And to get there, he followed the King's highway."

"I'm following," Buck said. "And I think I see where you are going. That suggests his future father-in-law was located somewhere around north Arabia and Transjordan, in a relatively safe region. Which also implies his encounter with the burning God on Mt. Sinai was not really in the Sinai Peninsula. So why is the name Sinai used if the mountain is not there?"

"Because Sinai is a region, and the Shara Mountain range, which is where we are now, was on the northeastern border of that region. The commonly accepted location for Mt Sinai is based on a 3rd-century attempt to locate the mountain, led by Constantine's mother. It's not grounded in local tradition; it's based on a Roman who had no real knowledge of the Hebrew tradition until she converted to Christianity.

"What is also relevant to the location of Mount Sinai is a phrase from the Book of Deuteronomy, relating Sinai to Seir. One phrase describes God's light rising from Sinai and shining on Sier. Another, in Judges, mentions that Yahweh came forth from Seir, advanced from the country of Edom. We know Edom was in this general region of southern Transjordan. And of course, this mountain range we call the Shara Mountains were once better known as the Seir Mountains. In other Old Testament books, such as Isaiah, god spoke to his prophet 'out of Seir'. Most believe this is a reference to God speaking from Mount Sinai – wherever that was."

"So," Buck concluded, "next you are going to tell me we are climbing The Mount Sinai?" He punctuated his questions by looking back at Kate with a raised eyebrow.

"No, I'm not going to tell you that. But I will point out one or two more things when we get to the top. You can tell me what you think later. And speaking of that, we are close."

Buck stopped and looked up. A long stretch of steep steps were cut into the rocky slope above, with rock walls off to either side. He could tell the steps leveled off up above. It looked like two small peaks might frame the area above.

Buck thought a moment and asked, "What will I see up there?"

Kate looked Buck in the eyes. "Let's wait till we get up there. I want to see what you think."

Buck nodded, "Sure. Let's get going."

The stone stairs ascended between natural rock walls that gradually formed two small peaks near the top of Jebel Al-Mahdbah. The peaks were connected by a broad, flat ridge. The northern, taller peak was to his right, and the southern was on his left. The path wound around the east side of southernmost peak and turned left, leading up between the two. Neither summit was impressive in terms of size, but a few things immediately caught his attention.

Ahead, the ridge between the peaks formed a flat sandy area. Off to his right, Buck could see another path with stone steps that wound up the north summit. Towards the top, stepped path went between the remains of ancient stone-brick walls. The walls obscured his view of the top.

Off to his left, the lower mountain peak had clearly been worked by stone masons. The top had been cut away, forming a flat platform. Angular walls had been cut into the side of the low peak, forming what looked like a small stone quarry on the front edge of the platform. Just over the upper lip of the quarry, on top of the man-made platform, Buck could see two roughly hewn obelisk-shaped pillars silhouetted against the bright blue mid-morning sky.

Buck and Kate paused, taking in their surroundings. Kate said, "As you can see, we aren't on a standalone mountain. These two small peaks are the summit of the Atuff Ridge, which connects the peaks of Jebel Al-Mahdbah with the surrounding Shara mountain range. The higher peak, to the north, overlooks Wadi Musa, or the Valley of Moses."

Kate seemed to take on a new energy. She took the lead and started up the right-hand path, almost running up the northern path to the ruined walls. "This way first," she called back to Buck.

"I thought we came to investigate the obelisks." He said as he caught up.

"Yes, but you should come up here first." They followed the path upwards and walked between the stone brick ruins. The ruined walls stood about twenty feet high and at least eight feet thick. "These walls were once thought to be part of a crusader fort. This structure is called Qasr el-Qantara, or the Citadel in English. The crusaders did occupy this area, but these ruins predate the crusaders by at least a thousand years. Most likely the bricks were cut from the quarry you saw behind us.

"The ruins were most likely part of an archway, or entrance to an even older worship complex. The complex is close - we are very close to the top now. It's really just above us, but the path is not direct."

Buck saw two obelisk-shaped pillars silhouetted against the sky

The path continued around to the right, or east side of the mountain's top, which was less than ten or twelve feet above their heads. The path ahead ended in a small open, flat area with a spectacular view facing north, over the Valley of Wadi Musa. As soon as Kate reached the open area, she took a sharp turn around to the opposite side of the peak, and faced the last rocky ascent in front of her. She climbed up the short rocky slope, Buck following behind her.

At last they stood on an oval-shaped plateau that stretched south, facing back in the general direction they had just come from. Kate walked confidently over the rough terrain, clearly confident in where she was going. Buck just caught up to Kate when he saw where she was going.

A large rectangular depression had been carved into the rocky ground ahead of them. It stretched about forty-five feet ahead of them, and was twenty-two feet wide, and about a foot and half deep. A bench-like border outlined the rectangle. On the west side, a rocky outcropping had been carved into an elaborate altar overlooking the valley below. Buck and Kate stepped down into the depression and walked towards the altar.

Just before the altar was a raised rectangle, about two to three inches high and roughly five feet long and two feet wide. It was placed at a right angle to the larger depression they stood in. It gave the appearance of a small stage, a place for some ancient priest to stand as he made use of the altar.

The altar consisted of two platforms, the nearest with three small steps leading up to a square stone surface with a rectangular depression in it. The second platform was a large flat rock with a depression in the top, and a small cistern carved into the side, fed by what appeared to be water channels carved into the surface. Both stood about three to three and half feet tall.

Kate walked up to the first altar and motioned Buck to follow. "This place is called the 'High Place of Sacrifice' today. Dad and I always thought it predates the Nabateans by more than a thousand years, but no one else really holds to that idea." She pointed straight ahead. "The mountain peak straight ahead - the further one, not the nearest – is Jebel Haroun, or the Mountain of Aaron."

"Aaron, as in Moses' brother," Buck said. It was more of a statement than a question.

"That's right. See the tiny white spot at the peak? That's the sun reflecting off of his tomb. I suspect it's not a coincidence this altar directly faces Aaron's traditional burial place."

Kate stepped back from the altar and led Buck towards the southern end of the plateau. They were now looking back over the ruined walls and the path down to the southern peak. Buck looked to the lower peak, it was clear the entire top had been removed to form a platform with the two stone pillars. Behind the pillars was a smaller, raised area forming a second, roughly hewn platform. A warm desert wind blew across the Atuff Ridge. Buck was suddenly struck with an odd feeling that this place was very old, older than the carved facades below, much older than anyone suspected.

"What is this place? It feels…. significant." Buck said. "I can't explain why I have that feeling, but I do."

"When Moses brought the Israelite elders to Sinai, he led seventy of them up the mountain and held a feast. Exodus says they ate and drank in God's presence. It describes God's feet standing on a floor or platform of something that looked like blue sapphire or bright blue lapis lazuli, depending on the translation. King James suggests it is sapphire, other more recent translations suggest lapis lazuli. All translations agree it was a precious blue stone. I prefer the way the King James Bible translates the verse. *'And they saw the God of Israel: and there was under his feet as it were a paved work of a sapphire stone and as it were the body of heaven in his clearness.'*"

Kate took a breath. It was clear she felt a connection to this story. "It was afterwards that Moses went up into a higher part of the mountain and eventually brought down the stone tablets."

"This mountains name, Jebel Al-Mahdbah, translates as 'Mountain of the Altar', or also 'Mountain of Sacrifice'. It was known as a holy place before the Nabateans settled here. Local tradition calls those towers, the two stone obelisks the 'Feet of God'.

"In recent years, archeologists have found evidence of lapis lazuli stone on the far platform, forming a floor, sort of a patio around the obelisks. With that in mind, I think it's really hard to ignore the similarities to the bible verse I just quoted.

"As a matter of fact, less than twenty years ago, a German archeologist named Ditlef Neilson wrote a book making the case that this is the location of the Biblical Mount Sinai. Very few scholars follow Neilson's line of thought, but that book is what brought me and my father here years ago."

Kate turned to look at Buck. "I wanted you to see this before we go further. This place had special meaning in ancient times, even predating traditional biblical historical periods. The Nabateans also recognized the importance of this location, and I think it still is a special place, perhaps even Holy is the right way to describe it.

"I can't explain it yet, but I am sure it's no coincidence that the search for the keystones is linked to this location. I'm not completely sure how, but it's somehow all tied together." Kate paused and looked back towards the obelisk-shaped towers.

"Let's go see what we can find on the other plateau."

Krause was seated near the truck's tailgate, his Mauser pointing in Jock's direction. "We should have had you and the woman at the Dead Sea. The secret exit your friend found was clever – but I knew we would catch up. It was obvious you were following the Professor's itinerary. The next logical place was where we actually took him."

Jock finally spoke up, in a demanding voice. "Emmitt Carter is alive? Where is he?!"

"So you will speak," Krause said. "Yes he's alive, but you won't find him. His daughter may yet see him alive, but not you. I have a use for her. After all, we need to make sure he talks before we are through with him."

"What is it you're after, Krause?" Jock spat out. "Some mythical artifact? I thought even you would have figured out these things can't help you by now. Himmler wasted years going after so-called magical objects, and none of it ever worked. The war is over – why don't you come to your senses and get on with life?"

Krause leaned forward, staring Jock in the eye. "This is different," he said in a quiet voice. "You have no idea what is truly going on here. The Jews that held these objects as sacred did not truly understand them. Once we have obtained them, we will be able to unlock an unheard of power. Power that only Herr Wolf can harness for a new age – A New Reich."

Jock stared back. "You're crazier than I thought."

Krause pulled his left hand back, as if to reply by striking Jock's face. Suddenly a sound from just outside the truck caught his attention. "We are not through," he said, turning to investigate. Krause opened the canvas flap and jumped out of the truck.

Jock heard sounds of a struggle, then a loud crack. 'What the hell is going on,' he thought.

A few minutes later, Buck was standing on the southern peak of Mahdbah, flanked by two stone pillars over 20 feet high. "I thought these were built, like the walls on the other summit. These look like they are actually part of the mountain itself."

"They are," Kate said. "Whoever cut away the mountain top intentionally left these in place, carving this platform around the pillars. That's an impressive feat no matter what time period it happened."

"If you're right about this being the original Sinai, then that predates Moses," Buck said. "That had to be thirty-two or thirty-three hundred years ago, right?"

"At least," Kate replied. "The Exodus story may even be older than that."

The ground around the pillars was strewn with natural debris – stones, sand and an occasional shrub. Some parts of the platform had clearly been carved to a flat surface. Erosion had taken an obvious toll on the ancient mason's work. Both pillars and platform displayed the effects of centuries of wind and sand beating against them. Behind the pillars, at the back of the platform was the raised area that formed the second platform. The east side had a lowered section resembling a very large step.

Buck shifted his focus. "Let's look for some sort of cave, doorway, tunnel or something. If this place is connected to the site in Palestine, I would think we should be looking for some kind of chamber near here."

Buck and Kate took opposite sides of the platform and started looking for anything that would indicate the presence of a chamber under the platform. As Buck neared the raised section, he asked "What was this structure?"

Kate looked over, shaking her head. "We never figured it out. It may have been some form of altar or podium for ceremonial purposes. We don't really know."

Buck climbed to the top of the platform. It was no different than the lower area. Tumbled rock, sand and debris covered the top. 'Podium is a good description', he thought. He scanned the rocky landscape to the rear of the platform. Jumbled, weather-worn sandstone sloped away from the platform.

Buck jumped down from the podium and walked to the edge of the larger platform. He was looking down at the path they followed up the mountain. There were sections of the mountainside cut away, forming a haphazard step-like structure down to the path. He turned back to face the podium-like structure. His eyes moved past the podium and scanned the ridge behind it.

About thirty or forty yards behind the obelisks and podium, slightly uphill and to the left, was an unusually flat spot nestled into the rocky landscape. It was flanked on the far side by natural rocky walls, fifteen to twenty feet high. A shadow in the wall indicated a recess.

He started picking his way across the ridge until he stood on the flat area. Kate followed him. Buck inspected the rock wall, and moved into the recess. It was roughly eight feet wide and just as deep. The back surface was unusually smooth, but did not offer any obvious signs of being man-made. Buck turned to look back towards the north. He realized the path up the north peak and the ruined walls were framed by the stone pillars. The altar on the High Place of Sacrifice wasn't visible, but he judged it would have been centered between and above the pillars if he could see it.

"I doubt that's a coincidence," Buck muttered. This small recess was too well aligned with the other landmarks to be entirely natural. He had a sudden thought. "This is probably a long shot, but let me see the Keystone."

Kate produced the crystal from her backpack and handed it to Buck. He felt the energy as he grasped the object, still amazed at the sensation. It seemed to be stronger than the sensation he felt in Quito. He realized that as he moved it closer to the smooth wall, the static-electric sensation seemed to gain intensity. Without any real plan or expectations, he slowly moved the Keystone towards the flat surface. The intensity of the sensation coming from the Keystone increased until his hand was slightly trembling. He looked at Kate. "Do you see that?"

She slowly nodded. "Yes – it looks like its reacting to something."

Buck held the relic about an inch away from the vertical surface, and started moving it back and forth, searching for a change in the Crystal's reaction. As he neared the center of the flat area, he decided to change tactics. Buck gently touched the Keystone to the flat surface. Without warning, a section of the flat wall trembled, and then stopped. It was if something had violently pushed outward from inside the rock wall. The sudden reaction nearly made him drop the ancient relic. Buck stepped back, examining the wall. A faint outline was now visible, exposed by the vibrations caused by the keystone. It was about four feet high and three feet wide.

Kate and Buck exchanged looks. "A door!" they said simultaneously.

Kate opened her backpack and took out a brush and a short pry bar, then quickly packed the Keystone away. Buck took the brush and started scrubbing the face of wall. A layer of sand and small chips of broken mortar started to fall away. The outline widened into a horizontal gap. Buck picked up the pry bar and used the sharp edge to chip away mortar, following the outline of the door downward on each side.

Buck placed the pry bar at the top of the door's outline, forcing it into the gap. He pushed upwards, trying to pry the top of the door out. "Stand back, this thing is going to fall hard," he warned Kate. The stone door started to creep outwards. He worked the pry bar deeper and pushed again. A six-inch-thick stone slab fell to the ground with a sharp crack. The sound echoed across the Atuff Ridge and surrounding mountains like a gunshot.

Kate put the brush and pry bar back in her pack, then produced one of Buck's military flashlights. She turned it on and pointed it into the darkness. Stale air and dust seemed to exhale from the dark opening. Once the dust cleared they could see an opening with shallow steps leading downward into darkness.

Kate glanced down at the stone slab and pointed. "Look at the back of the slab. It has a piece of crystal embedded in it. I think this has something to do with the reaction to the Keystone."

Buck examined the crystalline substance on the slab. "What the hell kind of material is that thing made of?"

Kate, shaking her head, had no answer.

Buck turned his attention to the entrance. He crouched and entered, Kate close behind. She handed Buck the light. The short flight of steps led straight down to a stone floor. Once at the bottom, Buck was able to stand. He swept the light from side to side. As their eyes adjusted to the low light level, they saw a man-made room that stretched thirty feet ahead of them, ten feet wide and at least twelve high. On each side of the room, about 5 feet off of the floor, a row of square recesses were carved into the rock walls, forming a series of small shelf-like holes. Jars, urns and tablets of various sizes and shapes sat in the shelves.

In the center of each wall, waist high stone platforms stuck out, forming roughly one foot by three foot tables. A third stone table was raised from the floor in the far end of the chamber. Behind that was a doorway into a second chamber. Buck could not make out anything through the open door, although it did not look as dark as he would have expected. "Is there a light source in there?" he asked.

"I don't know. Let's go further back," Kate said as she looked around. "The layout here seems vaguely familiar. I want to see what the far chamber looks like."

She took the lead and walked around the third stone table. The doorway was larger than the exterior entrance, about five feet wide by seven feet tall. As they approached the chamber's air seemed increasingly charged, as if it were saturated with static electricity. Through the door, the light seemed to throw a blue-white reflection off of an object in the back of the room.

 Buck directed his light at the ceiling and walls – no light was entering the chamber from outside. He judged the room was about ten feet by ten. He settled the beam of his lamp on the reflective object, eyes still adjusting to the changing light levels.

In the center of the room, a crystalline mass sat on a raised square stone pedestal. The pedestal was overly large for the crystal, almost as if it had been designed to support more than one such object. The crystalline itself was an identical twin to the crystal keystone that Kate had in her possession. As Buck eyes adjusted to the dim light, he realized it had no dust on it. The relic seemed to have repelled the dust that covered everything else in the chamber.

Out of curiosity, Buck switched off his light. A very faint blue-white light emanated from the keystone. "Incredible," he said out loud.

"Shh!" Kate hushed him. "I thought I heard something outside," she whispered.

Buck gave her the extinguished light, and motioned for her to stay put. He made his way through the dim outer chamber. Just short of the incoming sunlight he stopped to listen. Buck could just make out voices further down the ridge, speaking German. "Dammit," he said quietly. "Just like Palestine."

Buck crept back to the inner chamber, and quietly said to Kate, "You're right. Krauts are out there on the plateau." Looking around, he realized this was a dead end "OK… Not like Palestine," Buck whispered, his sense of urgency growing. "We need to get the key and get out. Unfortunately, we are probably headed for a fight. We need to move now. Make sure you have your gun ready."

"Great," Kate muttered, while Buck moved over to the pedestal. She opened her backpack as Buck grabbed the obelisk-shaped crystal. She heard a small electric 'crack!' and before she knew what happened, Buck lay unconscious on the floor, still grasping the keystone in his right hand. She looked in horror as she heard the voices echoing across the mountaintop outside the chamber.

Jock strained against the ropes around his wrists, trying to loosen them enough to slip a hand out. He knew that he had to get loose before Krause could come back. His hopes fell as the canvas flap in the rear of the truck was pulled aside. A large silhouetted figure stepped in. 'Dammit!' he thought,' Not enough time.'

A deep voice with a thick, unfamiliar accent startled Jock. "I'll cut you free. We won't have much time to get out of here before the damned Nazi awakes."

It was the stranger from the visitor's camp outside the hangar. "Who the hell are you?" Jock asked. "Not that I'm complaining, I could use a little help."

"My name is Aram Avakian. I can only tell you that your friend and the woman are in danger. I will help you get away, but in return you must abandon your quest for the crystal tablets and go home."

Aram pulled a large knife from his belt and cut Jock loose.

"Thanks," Jock said, rubbing his wrists. "Why go home? We came to find her father, not some tablets." He hesitated, and then added "you mean the keystones?"

Aram looked slightly amused. "Yes, the keystones. They do unlock something." Then his expression took a serious turn. "So you seek her father the Professor, and not the Stone?"

"Yes, Ms. Carter hired us to find him, so we are following along his trail, where he was last known to be. We aren't after any mythical relics, this is just our way to track him down."

"Then perhaps I can help you, but you must not try to recover the Stone. The tablets – or keystones, as you call them – were hidden for a good reason. They can unlock a dreadful power, one that has not been used for thousands of years. I am part of a society that has spent centuries ensuring these objects are not disturbed. We will continue to do so at all costs."

Aram continued as they climbed out of the truck. Krause was lying unconscious on the ground.

"Professor Carter is being held near Cairo. I know that he has held out against the Nazi's interrogations, but may not for much longer. They are camped in Giza, near the Saqqara Necropolis. Be warned, they have a small army and are well provisioned and heavily armed. When your friends make it back here, you must leave immediately. Do what you must to rescue him, there isn't much time."

Almost as an afterthought, Aram added, "I would much prefer to see that happen instead of the alternative."

"That was the plan," Jock replied. "Wait, what alternative? That almost sounds like you have something planned that puts his life in danger."

Aram responded in a very serious tone. "We only do what is necessary. I am giving you this information so you can accomplish your mission and save his life. I cannot offer much more help than that."

Jock knew when to stop pushing back. It was clear this man was giving them a break they needed. "What about Krause?"

"I'll bind him and leave him where he can't cause any immediate harm. I have no desire to kill anyone in cold blood, even a Nazi *aghmuk*."

Jock extended his hand. "Thanks," he said.

Aram shook it, and replied, "You must be warned. I cannot allow this Nazi to reach the Stone. The Covenant Stone is not meant for men like us to possess. I only ask that you remain focused on rescuing the old man and go back to America."

"Like I said, that's the plan," Jock said. "Look, I don't understand your role here, but I imagine we may need to cross paths again before this is over, and I personally owe you one. I obviously don't have the intel you do, but maybe we should maintain some form of contact. Is there a way we can reach out, just in case?"

Aram looked at him. "3.1 MHz. Use the call sign 'Seth'." Then he added, "Do not be surprised if we do not respond. There is more at stake here than you know, and we will not take casual risks for American mercenaries. Call only if it is truly unavoidable."

"You have my word."

Chapter 4 - Atuff Ridge, Shara Mountain Range - Transjordan

"Buck! Buck, wake up!" Kate's voice cut through the fog in Buck's head. He wasn't sure where he was. He opened his eyes, trying to make out his surroundings. It was dark, except for a very slight blue light. His head was pounding and ears ringing as if he had been hit with a baseball bat. Gradually Kate's face came into focus above him. Buck sat up. His entire body was sore, and his right arm was numb.

"What the hell, " he groaned. "What happened?" Buck rubbed his forehead. The pain was slowly receding, leaving a slight buzzing sensation in his head. He gathered his wits, and then bolted upright. "Nazis!" Buck stood up, steadying himself on the stone pedestal as he looked around. He shook off the fog in his head. He remembered grabbing the crystal keystone then feeling like he stuck his hand on a live wire. He shook his right hand, trying to force more circulation to get the feeling back. "Do you have the keystone?" he asked.

"Yes," Kate replied. "Are you OK? Can you make it?"

"Going to have to," Buck replied. He pulled his Ranger from his back holster, checking the chamber. "Get your pistol ready, and stay out of sight near the door. Wait for my signal and follow me. We'll have to move fast."

"Be careful..."Kate offered. Buck looked at her, shrugged his shoulders and crept to the front door, stopping while still in the shadows.

Buck gave his eyes a few seconds to adjust to the bright sunlight. The red-brown rocks and obelisk plateau lay slightly downhill, about thirty-five yards ahead. Beyond that the path that wound up to the higher peak. He could see a lone figure walking down that path, coming towards the obelisks. There had been two voices, so Buck assumed the other person was either on the far side of the stone podium, or in the lower space between the peaks. Just as the figure reached the bottom of the steps, he dipped out of sight.

"Now!" Buck hissed, and sprinted down the rocky slope towards the podium. Within a few seconds, he was crouching on the backside of the podium, listening. Kate hit the ground next to him. The sound of boots on stone carried from the far side. Buck removed his baseball cap, rolled it and stuffed it into his back pocket.

Buck looked up. 'Easy climb,' he thought. Buck slung the Ranger over his back and pulled himself up to the podium's top, careful to not make noise. He stayed on his stomach and crawled to the edge facing the stone pillars. Just below was a very large blond-haired man wearing a pistol, with a German Kar98K carbine slung over his shoulder. His back was to Buck. The first German had not made it up to the plateau yet. Buck realized he had to shift the odds in his favor by taking Blondie out immediately.

Buck pulled his legs under him, like a snake coiling for a strike. He jumped straight at the Blondie's back, hitting him square. The German hit the ground under Buck. Almost immediately, Blondie flipped around and was trying to pull Buck's shotgun free with his left hand. He had on a grip on the stock, pulling Buck close. His right hand reached for Buck's throat.

Buck countered by head-butting Blondie. Blood shot from the German's nose as he released Buck in surprise. Both men scrambled to their feet and squared off. Blondie went for his pistol. Buck reacted by grabbing the stock of his shotgun, and in a single motion pumped the handle and pulled the trigger. Buck's shot connected with the German's chest, knocking him back and over the edge of the plateau.

As Buck lowered his gun, he heard a German accent say "Hands up and drop the weapon!" Buck looked up, and the first German was pointing a pistol at him. "Slowly! Put the gun on the ground," the German commanded.

Buck set the shotgun down and slowly raised his hands.

A loud crack echoed across the Ridge as a round hole appeared in the German's chest. He looked down at the blood running down his shirt, then fell forward. Buck turned around, and saw Kate standing on the natural podium, both hands holding the Webley. Her face was white. "Did I really…" she started to say.

"Yes," Buck said. "You had to. You saved both our lives." Buck gave her a hand as she descended the rock formation. "We need to get down to the horses now."

Buck turned to the fallen mercenary, searching for anything useful. He took the Kar98k carbine, a Mauser pistol, and a two-way radio from the dead man's belt. He checked the magazine of both weapons – full. Buck put the safety on and tucked the Mauser in his belt. He handed the carbine to Kate. "Keep this."

Buck picked up the radio and turned it on, listening for traffic. He heard two voices conversing in German.

"Can you understand them?" Kate asked.

Buck nodded. "Sounds like 2 patrols checking in with each other. One is saying they found our horses. No mention of Ghaleb. He must've dodged them." Buck paused, listening. "The other patrol is in a place called 'Farasa', sounds like they have been searching on horseback for us. It sounds like they heard the gunshot, and are going to head back to where our horses are. They are trying to reach these two now."

Kate took a deep breath. "They are on both sides of us. Wadi Farasa is on the other side of this mountain ridge."

"If the second patrol is heading back to where we left Ghaleb, we might be able to wait them out and get away. Is there a way down into Wadi Farasa?"

"Yes," Kate replied. She looked at Buck. "You're bleeding."

Buck looked at the splatter on his shirt. "Not mine, that's from breaking Blondie's nose."

Kate shook her head, "No, you have a cut over your eye." She pulled a rag from her pack and wiped Buck's forehead.

Buck winced. "No time, need to go. Where is the other way down?"

Kate pointed to the west, almost directly opposite the path they followed up the mountain. "It starts just over there. I doubt the Germans are even aware of it. I remember that it's too difficult to climb up, since parts of the trail have been lost over time, but I think we can get down if we are careful."

Buck unrolled his reds cap and put it on. "Let's go."

As they started down the western face of Mahdbah, Buck reminded Kate to reload her pistol. The trail was passable for the first few hundred feet, and then became very rough. Some areas had eroded so badly they descend on all fours, sometimes sliding to a lower position on the mountain. Even with the difficult descent, they quickly made their way down to a spot just above the valley floor.

A pillared façade stood guard over the path zig-zagging up from the valley floor. In the shadows behind the pillars, a rough door lead into the ancient structure, offering a place to hide. Buck evaluated the next move. He stood just inside the door as he looked around the Wadi Farasa. Just a few yards outside the doorway, the valley floor was a sharp drop below. Below and to his left was a series of broken walls and pillars that offered some cover facing the valley floor. The path they followed down the mountainside was above and ascended to his right.

Buck turned his attention to the inside of the tomb. The walls had large carved niches, likely for burials. On the left was another doorway, leading into an even darker room. Kate was looking around and had pulled her lamp out to investigate the back room.

"Buck, someone has been living here." She pointed the light at the charred remains of a campfire and a few old, woven blankets on the floor. There was no sign of recent habitation. "Probably left from an old B'doul camp. I wonder if our pursuers chased them away?"

"Hard to say," Buck replied. "I need to see if I can get a bearing on the patrol." He switched on the confiscated radio. A static-filled conversation in German came through the speaker. Buck listened intently, and then shut it off. He turned back to the door, crouching just inside the shadows.

As Buck looked out he whispered, "I think the patrol is near – they mentioned nearing the end of the Farasa valley and heading back around to meet the others at the trail head. It sounds like there are two and they are on horseback." He turned to look at Kate. "We'll need those horses to get out of here. I need your help on this." Buck paused and added, "Again."

Kate took a deep breath. "What do you need me to do?"

Two German scouts were riding their horses north along the right side of Wadi Farasa, engaged in quiet conversation. The older scout was about a horse length ahead of his peer, and had been reminiscing about his days working in the Fuehrer's headquarters in Berlin. His younger companion kept his horse a bit to the rear to hide his obvious boredom.

The younger man was wondering how he could possibly change the conversation when he felt something strike his back. He turned in his saddle to see a woman step out from a large rock formation. She was wearing a dirty tan shirt and khaki trousers, and she was pointing a rifle at his head. She smiled at him, and placed her forefinger up to her lips, making a "shush" motion. His immediate confusion was replaced by the realization that she had him dead in her sights, and he probably couldn't get to his gun fast enough. He slowly raised his hands.

Suddenly, Buck stepped out at the top of the rocky hillside just ahead of them. He had his Ranger shotgun cocked, with the first of six twelve-gauge cartridges in the chamber and ready to fire. "That's far enough, Gerry. You're surrounded," Buck said.

The two Germans were caught from two sides, and they knew one move could mean a permanent end to their patrol. The older scout, showing some wisdom, also put his hands up.

A few minutes later, a lone horse made its way towards the mouth of Wadi Farasa. From a distance, it appeared to carry a large person wrapped in a tattered Bedouin sheet, wearing a makeshift keffiyeh, or Bedouin headdress covering his face.

Upon closer inspection, it might be clear the tattered sheet was covering a person of slight build, huddled against the riders back. As the two riders came around the northern spur of Jebel Al-Mahdbah, Buck realized that the impression of a lone rider would probably only be convincing when viewed from the front. He accepted that risk. His plan was not to sneak past the Nazi patrol at the foot of the mountain, but to surprise them.

Beneath the blanket, Kate pressed into his back, mentally preparing herself for a possible gunfight. She had her Webley and Buck's confiscated Mauser tucked into her belt, ready for a confrontation. She hoped it would not be necessary.

Buck's shotgun rested in his lap under the sheet, and the German carbine was tucked into a rifle holster strapped to the right side of the saddle. He gripped the stock as he anticipated their next move.

To his right, the rocky spur of Jebel Al-Mahdbah came to rest in the floor of the Valley of Moses. The dry stream bed that gave the Wadi Farasa its name wandered off to the left, into the open valley. Buck was aware of more ruins spread out across the valley floor, but could not allow himself the luxury of taking them in. Buck was sure they were bound for trouble ahead. Kate had explained the layout of the valley as they tied up the German patrol. He went through it in his head, working out what they might expect.

Buck knew that another patrol was waiting to join up with the one they had just ambushed. They were already on alert from the earlier sounds of gunfire, and by now had realized the scouts in Wadi Farasa were not able to answer their radio.

Once around the northern spur of Mahdbah, an ancient amphitheater would become visible. This was the northwestern end of the canyon they had entered from the Siq, with the ancient tomb facades lining both sides. From here, they would have a line of sight to the trailhead where they parted with

Ghaleb. The only question was how far this crude disguise would get them before the Germans recognize the deception.

Buck stopped the horse just before rounding the northern spur of the mountain to make sure they were both prepared.

"We're almost to the valley of the facades," he said quietly. "Once we turn to the right, it's only a matter of time. We need to maintain the illusion of a single Arab rider as long as possible. They are going to be watching, so we won't get out without a confrontation.

"We need to surprise them first, keep them off balance. When I give the word, drop the blanket and start shooting." Buck thought a moment, then added, "And hang on."

"I've never killed before today," Kate replied. "Now I may end up doing it again. I don't know what to think about that."

"It's hard, I know," Buck said. "But you have to remember that not only will these bastards kill us, but that your father's life is at stake too. If they engage us, remember that they brought it on." He added, "I know that's not much comfort. But it's all we've got right now, and we need to stay focused if we want to get out of this alive."

Kate nodded. "I'm ready," she said.

They remained quiet as they approached the end of the northern spur. Buck gently reined the horse to his right, and they entered the canyon of ancient tombs. The incredible grandeur of the valley before him, with massive carved buildings in the cliff walls to either side, would have been overwhelming in other circumstances. Buck narrowed his focus to the path he had to follow and continued to anticipate what might happen.

Just ahead to his right was the Roman-style amphitheater. Beyond that, over a quarter mile up the valley, he could see a small group of men and horses gathered near the trail leading up Jebel Al-Mahdbah. He knew they would be watching, waiting for their companions.

"Stay down behind me and be ready," Buck whispered. Buck nudged the horse into a light trot. He wanted to avoid rushing up on them, but also didn't want to give the Nazis too much time to see through their flimsy disguise. He said a silent prayer as they neared the amphitheater.

A group of five well-armed Germans stood with their horses next to the stone platform marking the trail up Jebel Al-Mahdbah.

One was listening to his handheld radio, trying to raise the patrol from the neighboring valley, with no luck. "Verdammtes radio!" he swore, looking around at the surrounding valley walls. "Diese Klippe Wände stören das Signal. <These cliff walls are blocking the signal.>"

One of his companions nudged him, gesturing down the valley towards the old amphitheater. A lone Arab horse and rider was trotting their way. The radio operator shook his head, wondering why they would pay attention to an Arab rider wandering through the valley.

The rider made his way closer. The German who first noticed him continued to watch, an uneasy feeling in his bones. Something was not right, but he couldn't put his finger on it.

Buck kept his shotgun tucked under the front of the blanket. He could feel the sweat flooding his palms, a sure feeling he was headed for a firefight. Buck had the first twelve-gauge cartridge loaded in the chamber, so his initial shot would not need the pump action. Kate kept her legs tucked up high, so her boots didn't hang below the fringes. She kept the Webley in her right hand, close to her stomach with the safety off.

Both were sweating under their makeshift disguise, waiting for the inevitable moment when one of the Germans would see through their flimsy cover. They were less than fifty feet from the group of German mercenaries. 'Closer than I thought we would get,' Buck thought. 'We'll spring it any second now.'

The German kept his eyes on the rider, now less than thirty feet away. He seemed unusually heavy for a desert nomad, with a very hunched back. He was armed as well, a rifle slung over the horses right side. The German unsnapped the holster containing his pistol as his uneasiness grew. He looked closer, squinting to try and bring the rider and his trappings into better focus. The rifle suddenly looked familiar – a German-army issued Kar98K. He slowly pulled his pistol from the holster.

Buck looked sideways at the men. They were about twenty feet away. One was fiddling with a handheld radio, three were looking the opposite direction, up towards the peak of Mahdbah, and the fifth was staring in Bucks direction. He had his hand on his pistol, slowly pulling it from the holster.

"Now!" Buck cried, kicking the horse while swinging his shotgun towards the four Germans. Kate swept the sheet off, the sudden burst of speed from their horse leaving the sheet suspended in midair. The next few seconds seemed to slow to a crawl as Kate pointed her gun towards the Germans.

The suspicious German pointed his pistol at them and fired. The bullet just missed Buck's head as his Ranger and Kate's Webley thundered back at the men. Buck's shot hit the man with the pistol in the chest. He fell backwards, knocking another man down. Kate's shot was a near miss, grazing the radio operator's shoulder.

Buck kicked his heels into the horse's side again, pushing it to accelerate. The remaining Germans scrambled to get on their own horses for the pursuit. By the time all four were mounted, Buck had his horse at full speed, heading up the valley.

The Germans were pushing their horses to catch up, and firing at the fleeing Americans. Kate felt/heard a bullet whistle past her head as she turned back and fired again. The gunshots echoed off the cliff walls around them. The pursuers were gaining as Al-Khaznah came into view. The narrow entrance to the Siq beckoned ahead to their left.

Suddenly a sharp crack of a rifle echoed from above, and the lead pursuer fell from his horse. Kate looked up in surprise. Buck glanced up to his left, just in time to see a dark figure dart behind rock on the cliff ledge above. "Ghaleb! He got away – Good man!" Without slowing, Buck waved his shotgun in acknowledgment.

Buck kicked his heels into the horse's side, pushing it to accelerate.

Buck urged his horse into the Siq, eager to lose the two remaining horsemen. He knew the narrow winding passage would offer some cover from gunfire, forcing them into a flat-out race to get as far ahead as possible – and being doubled up on a horse put them at a disadvantage. Buck realized their horse would tire faster than those of the pursuers.

The sound of galloping hooves bounced off the narrow canyon walls. Buck picked out the sound of the horses somewhere behind them, trying to judge whether or not they were getting closer. He turned his head to shout back at Kate, "If you see them, shoot – just make'em think about how close they get."

Buck dug his heels into the horse's side, pushing it harder. Kate fired off a few more rounds to keep the pursuers at distance as the canyon walls streaked by, not quite a blur. She thought there were times when she could have reached out and touched them.

Soon the rocky red walls opened up to either side, a sign that the outside entrance to the Siq was near. Buck knew that once free of the Siq's confines, they would be in the open for a good quarter mile stretch. After that, the road climbed up a long hill, then plunged down into the town of Wadi Musa. Buck hoped to use the maze-like streets to shake their pursuers.

Buck and Kate shot out of the Siq at top speed. Their horse swept past the B'doul campsite and over the stony bridge. They were now in the open as the road slowly turned to the left, climbing the long hill towards town.

The three German riders came out a few dozen yards behind them. Kate was ready and fired off a few more shots with the Webley. One of the riders clutched his chest and fell to the ground. Kate squeezed off the last round and tucked the pistol into her belt, exchanging it for the Mauser. She got off two more shots as they started up the hill. As she looked back, she saw one of the remaining horsemen falling back, apparently talking on a handheld radio. The other two kept their pace, slowly gaining ground.

"Buck, one more dropped back – we're down to two now." Kate said.

"Good," Buck replied, "Maybe we have a chance to evade these guys." They topped the hill, and Buck steered the horse down towards the winding alleys of Wadi Musa. By now he had holstered his shotgun across his back, and was focusing on pushing their steed to get into town.

The horse was working hard, starting to build up lather. 'He's getting tired,' Buck thought. He started down the main street away from the lost city of Petra, and then cut into a narrow alley on his right.

Suddenly, from one of the opposite streets, two motorcycles roared to life, following them into the alley. "Dammit!" Buck muttered. "They must've radioed for help." Buck pushed the poor horse harder yet, looking for an opportunity to lose the new pursuers. He took another right, doubling back around. The bikes missed the turn and were out of sight, temporarily. "Get off!" Buck ordered.

They dismounted, Buck grabbing the Kar98K as his feet hit the dusty ground. He slapped the horse on the rear, sending it galloping down the alley. Buck grabbed Kate, pulling her into the shadows of a recessed doorway. "Reload while you can," he whispered. "I'm betting they'll go after the horse before they realize we aren't on it – hopefully buy us a minute."

As soon as Jock parted with the stranger, he rushed to get back to the Goose. He prayed that Krause had not interfered with Abdullah's duties, and the plane would be fueled and ready. He ran across the air field as fast as he could. While Jock was no sprinter, his six-foot-five frame allowed him a long stride, and he set a good pace.

When he reached the Goose, Abdullah and the young boy from the hangar where coiling up the fuel hose. They stopped, looking at the large, slightly out-of-breath American in front of them.

"All Done!" Abdullah smiled. He walked up to Jock and put a hand on his shoulder. "You look a little tired, my friend. Perhaps you should have a seat and not exert yourself so much!" Jock sighed in relief, then shook his head and asked to settle up. Abdullah directed him to the manager's office to pay for the refueling services.

Shortly afterwards, Jock was back at the plane, preparing for two certainties. First, the plane needed to be ready to go at the drop of a hat. Jock ran through pre-flight checks as quickly as he could. Second, he knew that if Buck returned, it would be with company – and he had to be prepared. After the flight checks were complete, Jock went into the back of the Goose and opened a waist-high door in the port bulkhead. Jock looked at the small arsenal that he had built into the interior bulkhead of the goose. Jock scanned the collection of weaponry. He selected colt service revolver and a Lee Enfield Mk1 rifle with a 32MkII scope and a ten-round magazine.

'This should be good for some long-range cover' Jock thought. He picked up a few spare magazines and headed back towards the front of the Grumman.

From the cockpit, Jock took a moment to consider how the rest of the day might play out. He now knew where Emmitt Carter was being held, and even if Buck and Kate failed to evade capture that would probably become the next tactical objective anyway.

Jock knew he could be wrong, but he decided to trust that his best friend would make it back, although it would probably be in a running fight. After making the conscious choice to believe in Buck, he decided that preparing for a fast exit would be the best use of his time. Jock stepped back outside the Goose to scan his surroundings, thinking about what he might expect.

He expected that Buck would come from the northwest side of the airfield, which was to his left. There was no cover to speak of between the airfield entrance, marked by an administrative building and the hangar. The runway entrance ramp was just ahead, and was pointed to the East, more or less on Jock's right, an almost straight run onto the runway for a quick takeoff.

Jock judged that he had just enough room to taxi to his left to shorten Buck's route to the plane and still turn the Grumman enough to get back on the ramp for a quick takeoff if needed. There would be no coordinating with the airfield tower, but traffic wasn't really an issue here anyway. Jock removed the wheel chocks. Once he started the Goose's engines, he wanted to be able to move the aircraft quickly.

Jock climbed back inside the plane, leaving the hatch secured in the open position. He moved forward and sat in the left-hand pilot seat, sliding the side cockpit window open. Jock checked the Enfield's magazine and flipped the safety off. All that was left was to stay alert and wait.

Buck and Kate were huddled behind a makeshift fence at the side of a small building in the alley. Buck motioned for her to stay put, then pointed up to the top of the old building – he needed to get a view of the streets, to see where the motorcycles and other horsemen were. Kate nodded, indicating that she understood.

A small exterior flight of stone stairs went up the back side of the building to the second floor. Buck ran up the steps, and then used the stone door frame to help climb to the roof. Buck lay on his stomach as he scrambled from side to side, looking for their pursuers. His view of the crowded streets was limited, but the motorcycles would make enough noise and commotion that he believed he could estimate where they were and their direction.

The front of the building faced a main street, full of merchants and vendors. Cross streets to either side where narrow, but appeared to be active, with their own share of foot traffic and merchants. He could hear the drone of the motorcycles, one heading away down the main street, the other zig-zagging from one alley to the next, crossing the main thoroughfare, and methodically working back towards their hiding place. Buck noticed a flatbed truck with two European-looking men parked in the main street. The gauntlet was getting larger.

Buck saw the bike patrolling the alleyways cross two blocks down, and figured he had two, maybe three minutes to make a move.

He scrambled down the back steps and looked around their hiding spot. "What are you doing?" Kate asked.

"We need a ride out of here," Buck replied. He grabbed the Kar98K, pulled the bolt back and emptied the chamber. Kate looked at him with a question in her eyes.

"Have to do this with no gunshots," he whispered, motioning for her to stay hidden. Buck stood behind the corner of the building, listening. His hands gripped the barrel of the carbine like a batter about to step up to the plate. Buck knew he had to time this just right. He could hear the biker closing in on their position. Buck stepped out into the alley. He could hear he bike's wine as it accelerated towards him. He pulled the gun back to his right shoulder, his right elbow pulled as far back as possible. His left leg forward, weight centered over his right leg, Buck was in a power hitter's stance, working out the timing he needed to make this count.

'Now,' he thought. Buck's lower body started to shift forward, leading the way for his upper body to swing the makeshift bat in a savage swing, connecting across the oncoming motorcyclist's chest and shoulders.

The German biker flew backwards as his bike toppled and skidded down the alley. He hit the ground hard. Buck thought he could hear the air in the biker's lungs deflate from the impact.

"That's gonna hurt when he wakes up," Buck said, looking back at Kate. The carbine's stock had cracked and splintered, rendering the rifle useless. Buck dropped it, urgency creeping back in his voice. "Let's get that bike and get the hell out of here."

Buck picked up the bike, and scanned it for damage. He swung his leg over the seat and kicked the starter. Buck pulled his cap down tight as Kate grabbed her bag and jumped on the seat. As the bike accelerated, Kate huddled behind Buck on the seat. They took the alley running parallel to the main street, allowing them to get past the truck.

It was only a matter of seconds before the Germans realized their bike patrol had gone off plan – enough of an alarm to set them in pursuit. The truck swung into the alley behind them, locals scrambling to get out of the way as the Germans tore through the streets. Kate had her Webley reloaded and ready to provide cover fire, but didn't want to use it until they were clear of people.

Buck pushed the bike harder, opening the accelerator as he flew down the alley. The street twisted off to the left and downhill, forcing him to shift his balance for control. They needed to take advantage of the maze-like streets if they were to get away. "Hang on!" He shouted. Buck leaned into a hard right turn, using his leg to hold the bike up. He gassed the bike to speed down the connecting alleyway, then repeated the move to make a sharp left.

Buck picked alleys and streets at random, using the bikes speed and agility in the narrow alleys to lose the truck.

Jock heard the motorcycles engine screaming before he saw it. A single bike with two riders charged from the street side of the administration building towards Jock and the Goose. He was in the process of starting the Grumman's engines as a second motorcycle and a truck with two people appeared a few seconds later. He checked that the Grumman's brake was set, and then grabbed his Lee Enfield rifle. Jock positioned himself just inside the Grumman's hatch, rifle at the ready.

He saw Kate turn and open fire on the pursuers, forcing the second bike to slow down. The truck took the lead pursuit position, and the passenger leaned out, steadying a rifle around the truck's windshield.

Jock was already taking aim, and squeezed off a shot at the truck. It took out the windshield but missed the gunman and driver. His next shot hit the mirror, causing the driver to duck, veering off course.

The driver fought to keep it straight, following Buck and Kate. The German biker moved back to the front, gaining on the Americans. Kate turned, facing the biker and squeezed off two more shots, forcing him to think twice about getting too close.

Jock ducked into the cockpit and released the brake. He steered the Goose across the flight line, towards the runway. Buck saw his plane start to roll, and swung the bike to his right. He then steered in an arc to the left, bringing him parallel to the moving plane.

Jock was steering the goose back towards the runway entrance ramp. Once he had a straight shot to the ramp, he extended one arm out the pilot's window, holding the colt revolver. He squeezed cover fire out to give Buck time to get the bike close to the open hatch on the port side of the Grumman's fuselage.

Buck lined the bike up with the opening and shouted at Kate, "Jump!"

"Like Hell! Are you crazy!?!" she shot back without thinking.

Exasperated, Buck cried, "Yes! Now GO DAMMIT!" He opened the throttle, pushing the bike to get a little closer. He was within two feet of the plane's fuselage, fighting to keep the bike steady.

Kate realized it was the only way to get away from their pursuers, so she reached out to grasp the steel handle beside the open hatch. She managed push off of the bike and pull herself into the moving plane.

Buck looked back. The other bike was less than ten feet behind. Buck held the throttle steady, and stood up. He placed his left leg on the seat and held the throttle open. In one motion, Buck reached for the handle on the Goose's fuselage and pushed off the bike. For a moment he hung by his right hand as the Goose gained speed. Kate reached out and grasped his left forearm.

With Kate's help, Buck pulled himself up and into the plane. He looked back in time to see the abandoned bike wobble and fall directly in the path of the other motorcyclist, who crashed on the tarmac. The truck had to turn hard to avoid running the biker down.

Kate helped Buck shut and locked the hatch. Buck caught his breath, and turned to Kate. "You OK?"

She started to nod, then brushed the disheveled hair away from her face. "We really need to talk about your definition of OK."

Buck half smiled, realizing he liked her spirit. "That-a- girl," he said as he made his way forward. He could feel her eyes burning a hole into his back.

Buck took a seat beside Jock. Without speaking they increased the Grumman's speed as it started down the runway. In seconds they were airborne, leaving their pursuers behind.

Buck took a last look out the side window, the Shara Mountains glowing in the afternoon sun as they climbed to altitude.

Jock put a hand his shoulder. "So what happened out there? Looks like you stirred up a little trouble. "

Buck turned to Jock. "You should have seen that place. It was incredible. We confirmed that Emmitt was here. We also found the other key, but we still didn't find what we came for." Frustration crept into Buck's voice, "We weren't able to find out where her father is now."

"I know," Jock said calmly.

Buck eyed Jock, "What do you mean 'you know'. Why did you ask?"

Jock smiled, but with a grim demeanor. "I mean, I know where he is. You won't believe who I ran into..."

Chapter 5 - South of Cairo, near the Giza plateau - Egypt

The Grumman flew low over the Nile River, heading south from Cairo. As they neared the Egyptian capital, Buck made the decision to avoid the local airports. Both were still run by the American and British military, and allowed civilian traffic, but were also prone to observation. He anticipated the Germans would be looking for them in Cairo after the events at Petra. Both pilots searched for a suitable place to land the amphibious aircraft.

Jock spotted a small inlet on the west bank of Nile that offered seclusion. The inlet was surrounded by date palms and thick green shrubs. The entrance from the Nile was guarded by tall papyrus reeds, with an opening just wide enough to guide the Goose through.

Buck circled back and gently set the Goose down, the western shore to his left. He steered the plane towards the tall reeds near the shoreline, aiming for the gap in the reeds.

A few minutes later, they had the Goose anchored in a small, private harbor, and were setting up camp on a secluded beach. The location was reasonably secure, with no direct line of sight inland of the west bank of the Nile, and only marginal visibility from the river. The goose would provide secure enough sleeping quarters, no tent was needed. Jock started a small campfire and broke out some rations. After the day's events in Transjordan, any quiet meal was welcome, even canned beans, vegetables and potatoes.

During the meal, the three adventurers planned their next move. The first point of discussion was Jock's encounter with Wilhelm Krause and the mysterious Aram Avakian.

"Before Avakian showed up to spoil the fun, Krause made a few comments that stuck with me," Jock said. "I think he slipped a little, and not just in letting me know your father is still alive.

"First of all, it was clear they want you alive, obviously to coerce the Professor into talking. He must be pretty tough to hold out against that bunch. The fact that he's not giving them what they want is probably keeping him alive. It's also clear that we need to keep you away from them. If the Nazis get what they want, they'll have no reason to let either of you walk away."

"In fact," Buck added, "Knowing they are working more or less covertly suggests they would never allow a witness to talk about their operations. They're hoping to create a new Reich, so secrecy is paramount for them. Your Dad may be safe for the moment, but we will need to act soon. Krause will run out of patience." He looked at Kate. "I know that may be alarming to hear, but it's true. I expect we have a few days, but we still need to act fast. But we also need to be smart. We need to make sure we know as much about our enemy as possible." Buck turned back to Jock. "What else did Krause say?"

"For starters, that we had no idea what we were dealing with. Kate, you gave us the background on this stone he's chasing, and he seems to know that. That comment makes me wonder if they know something we don't. But the next thing really got my attention. Krause mentioned that this artifact has power, and I quote, 'power that only Herr Wolf can harness'. "Jock paused, and then said, "Do you think he's talking about..."

"Anything is possible," Buck replied. "We both know the Russian reports aren't reliable. Even if it is true, I don't think it changes anything for us. Krause is dangerous no matter who he's working for. He is our immediate problem."

Kate broke in, "Can you say more about this Aram Avakian? What did he look like?"

"What are you thinking, Kate?" Buck asked.

"I am wondering if he is the second visitor we had, the one with the warnings. Was he tall, dark hair, with a mustache?"

"Yeah," Jock said, "He also spoke with a heavy accent – I couldn't tell what it was. Does that sound like your visitor?"

"Yes," she said. "So he's obviously not with the Germans... Who is he?"

"He seemed to be willing to help me as long as we were more interested in your father than the artifact. He basically suggested he was part of some group that was protecting it from outsiders. It seemed clear that they don't want to harm us, but only if we focus on your father. Then when I asked him about staying in contact, he gave me a radio frequency and a call sign, 'Seth'.

"He also seemed to believe this artifact, the Covenant Stone, holds some terrible power. He was every bit as convinced as our German friends. Regardless, we know we don't want the Germans to get it. There may be a way to partner with these guys."

Buck interjected, "You're right, but our focus is her father over the artifact. So let's focus on that first. This Aram person said Professor Carter is being held near the Pyramids?"

"He mentioned a place called 'Saqqara'," Jock replied. "I've never heard of it."

Kate took the cue. "I know where that is. The Giza plateau and the desert south of it are home to more than just the three Great Pyramids. Besides the three that most of the world is aware of, there are other, older structures. The Saqqara Necropolis contains several of those older pyramids and is one of the oldest known burial sites in Egypt.

"The site of the Three Great Pyramids is on the actual plateau, just outside of Cairo. Saqqara and the older pyramids are about twelve miles to the south. These older pyramids were basically prototypes for the larger ones you know of. The necropolis of Saqqara is as old as the Egyptian civilization. The city of Memphis was built on the older, perhaps first, capital city of early Egypt. The kings and nobles of the very first dynasties used this area for their burials, as did many of the subsequent dynasties. Some parts of Saqqara are at least five thousand years old, maybe more.

"Dad always suspected a connection between early Egyptian civilization and older Sumerian culture. Maybe that's why they are at Saqqara – and maybe the Nazis believe the Covenant Stone is nearby. One thing I haven't quite worked out is why the Keystones seem to be popping up in places that seem to be connected to more recent Hebrew history."

Buck added, "The modern settlement built near ancient Memphis is close. We flew over it as we were searching for a place to land. This puts us in a good place to do a little reconnaissance."

Kate asked, "What's the plan? I want to get going."

Buck looked up at the darkening sky. "It's almost sundown. After nightfall I think I'll do some scouting, and learn what I can about their location, and if I'm lucky, resources. We need to get some information before we jump into a rescue mission. I'm expecting this will take some planning on our part – the more we know, the better."

Kate started to speak, but Buck interrupted her. "You should stay." She shot him an indignant look, but he continued. "I know you can handle yourself. Regardless, it's clear from Krause's comments that they want to use you to break your father. We can't let that happen. I will need your help in another way though."

The night sky was crystal clear. A lone rider in Arab clothing picked his way up the long slope leading out of the lush Nile valley. It was the second time in a day that Buck was using local Arab garb to hide his identity. The stars provided good light as Buck made his way onto the higher desert landscape holding the oldest structures known to man.

His colt was hidden beneath the white robes. Buck decided to leave the larger firearms behind. He had no desire to risk unnecessary attention from distant onlookers. Instead he carried a compass, binoculars and a map inside a small pack slung on the camels saddle. As he topped the slope onto the Giza plateau, Buck paused to get his bearings.

A few hours earlier, Kate used Buck's navigation maps to get their bearings in relation to the Saqqara Necropolis. As luck would have it, they were near a small town built on the remains of ancient Memphis, so locating and renting a camel and purchasing local garb didn't take long. Buck paid what most would consider an outrageous amount for the use of the camel for the next few hours, but he wasn't about to lose the deal considering the stakes.

The moonlit sand stretched for miles to the North, East and South around him. Behind Buck, small lights punctuated the darkness, highlighting settlements along the Nile Valley. A warm breeze brought the smell of the river up, surprisingly similar to the nighttime smells Buck experienced when trekking through the Amazon basin.

Buck turned his attention to the map and compass. If he had his location right, the necropolis would be to the north, featuring a prominent, two hundred-foot high stepped pyramid. Near the stepped pyramid would be several smaller pyramid-like structures, most of which were so deteriorated they simply looked like a pile of rubble. Around the ancient pyramid complex a field of tombs, usually inside the remnants of ancient *mastabas*, or square, mudbrick crypts, extended for a several square miles. This field of ancient tombs would provide a small amount of cover that should allow Buck to scout out the Nazi camp.

Kate had remarked that most were still not excavated, so they really had no idea how extensive the necropolis actually was. Many of the tombs in the area were extremely old, from the first known (possibly founding) dynasty of the Egyptian civilization. Other tombs in the area were also from subsequent dynasties, implying the assumed extensive nature of the necropolis. The landmark stepped pyramid was from a later dynasty (probably the third) and was believed to have been designed by the famous architect and physician Imhotep, for the King Djoser. It served as a precursor to the Great Pyramids, the gigantic structures Buck had only seen once before, during his brief military tour in North Africa.

Buck studied the map, and then looked around the moonlight desert landscape. A very faint glow over the rocky ground to his right was visible. The necropolis should be almost directly north, so Buck decided to head west for about a mile, then turn right and swing around to get a look from the other side. His thought was that if anyone saw him in the distance, it would look like a Bedouin heading north from the desert towards Cairo, instead of someone scouting the area coming from the populated town of Memphis.

Buck put the map away and took the camel straight east for abut twenty minutes, and then turned to his right. He went another mile or so then swung east, to approach the Necropolis from the desert side. The glow was just ahead and a little to his right – he was slightly north of the lights, but still too far out to get a good look at the source. All he could really tell was that the lights seemed to be reflected by a structure behind them.

Buck steered the camel closer, and soon realized the light was coming from an encampment at the base of a large step-sided pyramid. It had to be the structure Kate described. The pyramid was about two hundred feet tall. To the right, or south, was a large courtyard surrounded by low ruined walls. On the near side, at the western base of the pyramid, several small tents were visible. On the far side he could see more ruins, but they were too far away to make out any details.

The ground around Buck was hilly and uneven, and the rough terrain offered the expected cover. Buck steered the camel behind a low rise and uttered the commands the camel's proprietor taught him, " 'Asfal! (Down!)," and "Albaqa'! (Stay!)." He dismounted and untied his pack from the saddle.

The owner had insisted this camel was exceptionally well behaved and obedient, but Buck had his doubts. His previous experience in North Africa indicated this was usually not the norm, and Buck was worried his rented steed would wander off while he crept up the hill to get a better look at the encampment.

Buck lay on his stomach at the crest of the small hill, binoculars trained on the lights. The Step-sided pyramid towered above a collection of gray-green tents and several vehicles suited for desert travel. Buck scanned to the left of the pyramid and took stock of the vehicles; four jeeps, three trucks large enough to be small troop carriers and three motorcycles, in a small open area surrounded by low, crumbling walls.

He swung the binoculars back to the tents. Buck counted seven small barracks tents in the outer row, arranged in an arc at the base of the pyramid. He estimated each tent would house at least four men. There were three larger tents in the middle. The lights Buck had noticed earlier were arranged around this central area. Of the three, the left-most tent had several long tables and chairs outside, with a handful of men eating a late meal. The tent on the right had a large portable generator running outside the tent, obviously running the lights. Buck was also able to see into the entrance, and detected some electronic equipment inside – probably communications gear. The center tent was unique in that it had two stationary guards outside the entrance.

There wasn't much activity except for the people eating and a few others inspecting the vehicles. It was late enough that Buck expected most were getting some sleep. Buck saw a large man walking out of the communications tent and walk towards the central tent with the guards. He recognized the man immediately. 'Krause is already here,' he thought to himself. 'He didn't waste any time.'

The guards snapped a salute as he approached. Krause returned the salute, and one of the guards pulled the entrance flap open. Krause entered and the flap closed behind him. 'Not hard to guess who's in there,' Buck thought with satisfaction. He now felt like they had a line of sight on their target and while the ten-to-one odds presented obvious difficulty, some creative tactics might allow them to free Professor Carter if they could act quickly.

Buck started to put his binoculars away when the drone of engines reached his ears. He pulled them back out and started scanning the landscape. He soon saw several more vehicles were approaching over the desert, from the northwest. Buck took a quick count. "Son of a bitch!" he muttered. There were eight uncovered troop trucks each full of men, followed by a large supply truck, probably carrying more tents and gear for the new arrivals.

The convoy circled around to the north side of the pyramid and parked. Buck watched as men jumped out of the back of the trucks and started to unload several wooden crates.

Buck saw an encampment at the base of a large step-sided pyramid

Buck estimated eight to ten men in the back of each. He watched long enough to take stock of their cargo; more tents, lights, supply crates and makeshift barricades. The men were carrying light weapons, clearly used to being mobile.

Buck soon had a good idea for how they were provisioned. Krause's outfit had well over a hundred men – a small company in military terms. The Nazis meant business, and clearly expected something to happen soon.

Buck also noticed the convoy had approached from the less populated region west of the Nile, to avoid unwanted attention. Buck was a little surprised they had this level of organization so soon after the end of the War. He began to feel sick to his stomach as he watched. This had gone from bad to worse very quickly.

Buck crawled back down the hill, slightly relieved to find his ride sitting on its haunches, still waiting. He mounted the camel and started to retrace his path. This was going to a lot harder than he had hoped.

"We need help." Buck, Jock and Kate sat around their small campfire as the morning light broke over the Nile. The rations that made up breakfast did little to ease the feeling Buck had in his gut. As they ate, Buck walked the others through his observations from the previous night. He could see the same feeling was beginning to take hold for Jock and Kate.

Jock spoke first. "A company's worth of men…. We've been outnumbered before, and outsmarted and outfought them – but those odds are next to insane"

Kate replied, her frustrated growing. "We can't give up. We are too close! There has to be away to get Dad away from them." She paused, "Maybe we should just give them the keystones."

Jock shook his head as Buck spoke up. "No. It looks like your Father is holding out for a reason. We need to keep that in mind. And anything that gives these bastards a step up is usually bad for everyone else."

Buck looked her in the eye. "We are going to rescue the Professor. We may have an ally nearby."

Jock nodded, and spoke one word. "Asad."

"Yes. We need to pack up and head into Cairo. There used to be a marina on the Nile where we can park the Goose. It's busy enough I think she'll be safe while we visit Asad.

Kate looked back and forth between the two men. "Who is Asad?"

Buck proceeded to give her some background about the man they were going to see.

"Asad is a dangerous man. Let's just say, he operates by his own rules. He has a lot of resources and a lot of pull in the Cairo underground, and during the war was active as far west as Morocco. In fact, he helped us break a network of Nazi spies, which was instrumental in the success of Operation Torch. Asad's help was instrumental in pushing Germany back from Northern Africa."

"So we can trust him, right?" Kate asked.

"At heart, Asad's a nationalist. He wants Egypt to be an independent state, out from under Britain and with its own, self-sustaining government. Asad has no love for the British, because from his point of view, they have essentially occupied his homeland for a long time. And sometimes that dislike extends to their Allies. He is also disillusioned with Egypt's leaders, because of the perceived reliance on the British.

"But the bottom line is that Asad has an extreme hatred for the Nazis. They were responsible for the death of his family when Germany invaded North Africa. I never learned all the details, but that was the basis for the help he gave us four years ago. So I think we can trust him to help us hurt anyone that is a part of the Nazi movement."

"That isn't the same as trusting him to help save my father," Kate replied.

"No, but I do believe he is an honorable man. Still, he is what we could call a gangster back in the States. He operates outside of the law here in Cairo, so we need to be cautious. Considering how well staffed these Nazi bastards are, I think he's our best chance."

"I hope that's enough," Kate said.

Asad Madboury Shadid sat across from Buck and his companions in a small, ornate coffee shop in the Khan el-Khalili souq in downtown Cairo. The crowded street outside the shop entrance was filled with people bartering for the best deals on goods such as linen, clothing, and food, not to mention some more questionable goods and services. The sounds of the marketplace drifted into the shop as Asad smiled, assessing the three travelers in front of him. His short black beard framed his narrow, eagle-eyed face. He was dressed in a white business suit. 'The months since the war have been good to him," Buck thought.

"To what do I owe this unexpected pleasure, Captain Haggard? Or should I just say Mister Haggard?"

"I'm a civilian now," Buck said. "And I won't waste your time, Asad. I'll get right to the point. We need your help, and we are desperate. You're the only man I know in Cairo who may have the connections to help us."

"Ahh, you are, as always, direct." Asad replied, a slightly amused look on his face. "What is it you are looking for?"

Kate looked back and forth between her companions and the Egyptian. Buck and Jock were essentially expressionless, where Asad seemed amused. Kate sensed some tension between them. It was clear that they needed this man and his resources, but as far as she could see, had little to no leverage. Buck had advised them to let him do the talking, since he had the most experience with Asad. They were happy to let him take the lead.

Buck leaned forward in his seat. "This young lady's father is being held prisoner in a large camp of well- armed men in the Saqqara ruins south of here. We need to get him out– tonight, if possible."

Asad's eyes narrowed. "I've heard about the camp in Saqqara, but have heard very little about who they are or why they are there. I assumed them to be some group of foreign mercenaries." Asad took a sip of his coffee, and then leaned back in his chair. "So tell me, what is your involvement with them, and why do they have this woman's father with them?"

"Ms. Carter hired us to find her father, who went missing on an archeological dig in Jordan. He was researching an ancient, very valuable artifact that these men want to take. I believe they intend to use it to finance a very dangerous enterprise. Her father, Professor Carter, was very close to uncovering the location of this artifact."

"So he is a treasure hunter?" Asad paused. "I am not interested in helping anyone dig up and take treasures from Egypt, or anywhere else in the Arab world."

Kate started to respond, but Buck put his hand up. He continued, "Let me back up. Neither we nor the professor want to 'take' anything. However, in the course of his studies, the Professor found evidence of an artifact that may, in fact, be connected to very old stories common to Bible and the Koran. His goal was to prove its existence, but he had no intention of taking or keeping this for himself. I believe his intention was to find the item, then turn it over to whatever sovereign country it was discovered in. This man is an academic, not a treasure hunter. He is chasing truth, not treasure."

"As far as this 'treasure' is concerned, it's not some cache of gold, it's an artifact that may be connected to stories in Genesis, and probably offers some proof of the historical truth in our common beliefs. If that holds true, this thing could be extremely valuable in some circles.

"Just so we are clear, I am not interested in whatever this thing is – my objective is to rescue the Professor, and if possible, keep these men away from his research. I believe that if this artifact does exist, this thing is probably extremely valuable and can at least bring a good price on the antiquities black market. I think that's where these mercenaries as you call them, come into the picture."

Asad crossed his arms. His brows furrowed as he said, "In my experience, mercenaries never take the initiative to do things like this arbitrarily. There is always someone else paying for them, and that may be of greater concern. Before I decide whether or not to get involved, I have two more questions. First, what is this object, and second, can you tell me who the mercenaries work for?"

Buck replied, "I'll let Kate answer the first question."

Kate took her queue, relaying a condensed version of the background she gave Buck two weeks earlier. "The artifact in question is supposed to an ancient talisman or powerful device that can be used to build up or destroy things, or structures. Legend says it was used in the construction of the Tower of Babel, and misuse caused the tower to collapse. Dad found references in ancient Babylon, from a time that predates most of written history. There are other, older non-biblical references that suggest it was used in the construction of Noah's Ark. After the tower story, it apparently disappeared. However, Dad later found some evidence that it had made its way into Palestine. He disappeared shortly after a visit to the Dead Sea. We picked up his trail there, which led us to Transjordan. In Petra, we found out he was kidnapped and brought here."

"So these mercenaries brought him to Saqqara? They obviously have reason to think this object is here," Asad responded. Kate could see he was working out whether or not the artifact was fair game for him. She wasn't surprised by that thought. According to Buck, Asad was a bit of a mercenary himself.

Buck sat back, looking Asad squarely in the eyes. "I never said these men were mercenaries. Remember, that was your term.' He paused. "They are a remnant of Nazis, and I think they intend to use this artifact to finance renewed operations between Europe and South America."

A shadow fell over Asad's face. "How many men do you need?"

In less than an hour, all four had relocated to Asad's residence in old Cairo, only a short ride in Asad's car. They followed Asad into a walled compound near the west side of the old city. The house at the center of the compound was a tall three-story building that served as Asad's home and his base of operations. Asad had three of his lieutenants join them in a private meeting room on the top floor, overlooking a pool and patio area surrounded by palms. The apex of great pyramid of Cheops was barely visible in the distance, across the Nile and beyond the sprawling urban growth of Cairo.

Kate forced herself to ignore the massive structure and pay attention to the almost conspiratorial conversation around her.

A hand-drawn map of the Saqqara Necropolis was on the table. Buck and Asad were discussing the best ways to approach the main Stepped pyramid, where cover was available, and the German camp layout. The atmosphere was one of nervous energy and anticipation, like a war room.

As they all took a seat around the table, Buck looked at them, scanning their stoic faces. "Are you sure this is a fight you all want to be in?" Asad's three companions had clearly put their trust in Asad as their leader, and seemed ready to take up arms at his command. Regardless, Buck wanted to make sure they were all on board. He knew that loss of life was a probability.

Asad nodded. "We all lost something to these Nazi rats. Any chance to pay them back is a gift from Allah." His men all voiced their approval.

"Good," Buck said. "And we are in your debt. Now let's talk about how we pull this off." He turned his attention to the map.

Asad's men allowed Buck and Asad to do the talking, only interjecting where their respective areas of expertise were needed. Buck walked them through his observations from the previous night, noting placement of vehicles, tents and supplies.

As much as Asad wanted to aggressively attack the camp, he was not able to muster enough men to take on a small company. The group agreed the best approach was a guerilla-style attack on the northwest side of the camp, providing enough distraction for Buck and Asad to infiltrate the camp. The camp was set up against the west side of the stepped pyramid, and the parking area for the vehicles was on the north side.

Buck and Asad would approach from the East, using the rough terrain and ruins of the necropolis as cover. As the attack starts, the plan was to go around the south side of the pyramid and enter the camp from the south. Jock would find a position to the Southwest, where he could observe Buck and Asad's movements from a distance. He would signal the main attack force to engage and retreat, based on Buck and Asad's progress. He would also have his sniper rifle, and be ready to provide cover fire if necessary.

"We need to expect resistance, especially once the Nazis get over the initial surprise," Buck said. We need an exit where we can take cover without getting pinned down."

Asad pointed to the south end of the Pyramid complex. "As we leave, go to the old wall on the south. There is a colonnaded path leading to the East."

Hakeem, a tall Nubian, responded. "We have several of your country's old M2 60mm mortars. We can use them in the assault. We can also position one to launch phosphorous shells and provide smoke cover for the retreat."

Buck nodded. He recognized Hakim from the Morocco Operation four years earlier. He was a strong, dependable fighter. "What about the frontal attack? Can you keep them occupied long enough for us to get in from the other side? We can't get into a full-on fight, but the attack needs to aggressive enough that all their attention is focused to the northwest. And your men need to be able to retreat safely once we get the Professor out."

A small wiry Arab named Ibrahim, who looked like he had spent his entire life in the Sahara, spoke up. "At the outset of the attack, we will use the mortars to damage their vehicle fleet, as well as their entrance to the vehicle staging area on the northwest side. They will not be able to pursue us, unless it is on foot. Any transport we do not destroy will not be able to leave."

Jock had been quiet through most of the discussion. He broke his silence with a statement. "We need to think about two more things. First, Buck's retreat once we have the Professor out, and where to go. Even if the Nazis can't follow right away, they will want to retaliate. Second, we need to keep Ms. Carter safe both during our attack and afterwards. Krause made it clear she was as valuable to them as the Professor."

Asad replied, "This compound is very well protected. I have men standing watch. They will signal us in case of any reprisal."

Buck added, "I'm sure that once we have Professor Carter free, we will still have some work ahead of us to make sure we can get him home safely, but the first order of business is to get him out of there, then look into how we can make sure both of the Carters stay safe."

Kate realized she hadn't actually thought of that. What would prevent the Nazis from coming after her or her father again?

Buck saw the apprehension on her face. "One thing at a time," he said. "Rescuing your father will cause some disruption and slow them down, and hopefully hurt them enough to delay their operation. These rats don't have unlimited resources, but they will retaliate in some way. We may just need to get you and your father to safety before they can regroup enough to try anything."

"I wish that made me feel better," Kate said. "What can I do to help with the rescue?"

Asad shook his head. "You are too valuable to risk in the operation. As Captain Haggard has said, we need to keep you safely away from the Germans. You will stay here with a small contingent of armed guards to keep you safe."

Kate nodded. She understood but didn't like it. The experience at Petra had taught her she could hold her own, even if she lacked the experience of these men.

Buck rolled up the map. "Let's start getting our supplies and men organized. We still have a lot of planning to do, and this is going to be a long night. Let's talk about the diversion and the attack."

Jock lay on his stomach with a short-wave radio at his side. The evening light was almost gone, and he could see clouds beginning to gather on the horizon. 'This might actually only help our cause tonight,' he thought to himself.

Jock was about 900 yards away from the Saqqara complex, taking cover behind the rubble on a small ridge. Just a few yards to his left, Hakeem was setting up a mortar behind a ruined wall. Jock turned his attention to Hakeem. "Do you have the phosphorous shells?"

Hakeem nodded, "I have plenty. We will give Buck and Asad good cover tonight."

Jock gave him thumbs up, and then turned his attention back to his Lee Enfield No. 1 Mk III, equipped with a telescopic sight. The rifle was pointed towards the pyramid and wrapped in tan burlap strips to prevent any metallic glare that might be spotted by their enemy.

Jock used the rifle's scope to scan left to right, starting on the north side of the stepped pyramid, across the camp. Jock noted that instead of the single semi-circle of barracks tents Buck had described, the newly arrived troops had put up an additional line of tents, expanding the camp's foot print. Jock continued his scan of the area, sweeping over the open courtyard to the south of the pyramid and ending at a line of pillars and that extended almost straight East from the courtyard towards the town of Memphis. The only part of the camp he didn't have a good line of site on was the northernmost open courtyard where most of the vehicles were parked. Jock could see a portion of that area, but if things went as planned, he had no need to see it.

The southern courtyard and the ruined walls were Buck and Asad's entrance and exit routes to the Nazi camp, and where Jock expected to provide cover fire as they retreat. He was also in a position to relay a signal to Asad's men who would attack from the northwest side of the camp, offering a vital distraction that would allow Buck to sneak in, find the professor and exit.

Jock was the lynchpin of the operation, observing and coordinating between infiltration, attack and retreat. He had played this role many times in the past, but never expected to do this after the war ended; of course, he had not expected to ever run into a company of Nazis again. Jock ran through the plan in his mind as he waited for night to fall.

To the north, a group of twenty-three of Asad's men was on horseback, staying under cover and out of site until the signal was given. They would provide the primary visible distraction, drawing the German forces to the north side of the camp.

Spaced at even intervals around the camp, about 1500 yards away from the pyramid, Asad had placed five more men with light infantry M2 60mm Mortars. While the men to the north would provide a visible distraction and target, these men would rain thunder down on the perimeter of the camp, effectively doubling the impact of the attack, and pinning the Germans down enough to allow everyone else to retreat.

They would also target the vehicles and transport staging area, which was critical to pulling this off. A clean getaway relied on pinpoint accuracy of the mortars. One of the mortars was equipped with phosphorous or white smoke shells that could be used to create confusion and give the infiltrators additional cover. After the retreat, Jock would be picked up by the mortar gunner closest to him.

These five men would be the last to leave, also on horseback. They probably had the most dangerous job next to Buck and Asad.

This was designed to allow Buck and Asad to sneak in while the Germans backs were turned. The ruse would only be effective for a very short time. One mistake or delay, and Buck and his Egyptian counterpart could be dead.

Half a mile down the hill towards the Nile valley, a small truck would be waiting for Buck, Asad and the professor. All of the participants were to head in separate directions, then rendezvous at the compound in Old Cairo by morning.

Jock settled in, trying to get as comfortable as possible. He still had a few hours left before the show would start.

Nightfall had finally come, and the darkness was complete. By some apparent act of providence, clouds obscured the sky, blocking the starlight. On the southeastern side of the Pyramid, Buck and Asad crept forward through the outer edge of the necropolis. Both men were dressed in black and lightly armed, Asad with a knife and a Webley automatic Mk1 holstered to his belt, and Buck with his colts strapped to each leg. He also had a small survival knife tucked into his belt.

They slowly and quietly made their way towards the stepped pyramid and the surrounding ruins, watching for the inevitable German foot patrol. As they paused beneath a pile of tumbled blocks, Asad took a moment to look around. He motioned to Buck and pointed towards the remains of a wall ahead of them, about twenty feet high. The wall had once been part of a fortification that once surrounded the Saqqara pyramid complex.

A door punctuated the center of the wall, a rectangle of blackness that led towards their objective. At the top of the wall, the silhouette of a man stood guard. His vantage point should have allowed him to see anyone approaching from the East, but the nearly total darkness had provided enough cover for Buck and Asad to get close.

Buck checked his watch. They had less than 10 minutes to get into position, which meant taking out this guard and getting to the other side of the temple wall. He looked at Asad, and whispered "10 minutes – we need to move fast."

Asad looked at Buck. "I have this,' he quietly replied, patting the sheathed knife in his belt. He quickly disappeared into the shadows between the ancient rubble. Less than a minute later, Buck heard a short scuffle, then a grunt. He looked at the top of the wall, and saw the faint outline of a man waving in his direction. Buck made for the doorway in the wall.

Asad met him at the entrance. They entered a twenty-five yard long colonnaded corridor. The walls on both sides were open, and only remnants of a roof blocked out the night sky. Uneven piles of rubble lie on both sides of the corridor, providing minimal, but useful cover. When they reached the end of the corridor, it opened up into a courtyard facing north towards the stepped pyramid. The remains of the surrounding wall provided some cover on either side of the courtyard. Asad and Buck took cover between the pillars, looking towards the great stepped structure. The courtyard was open, with low walls running on either side, forming a great rectangle with the pyramid in the center. Buck could see the glow of electric lights illuminating the left side of the five thousand year old stepped structure.

Buck motioned Asad to follow. He moved quickly behind the right-hand wall, staying low and in the shadows. The men stopped as they reached the base of the pyramid, taking cover in the shadows.

From here, the plan was to wait for the light show, and then Buck would move west along the pyramid's base and enter the camp from the south side. Asad would break off and take cover behind the ruined wall to their right. From here, he could provide cover fire and disrupt any resistance as Buck made his way back with the Professor. Buck and Asad knew that Jock should be watching them with his sniper scope, along with activity within the camp, and he would radio a signal to Asad's men when he was satisfied the time was right. They didn't have to wait long.

A single low whistling sound from above the camp signaled the start of the attack. The mortar shell exploded as it impacted the ground just north of the camp, skillfully placed to minimize damage to the ancient ruins. More whistling and accompanying explosions materialized in a matter of seconds. Buck sprinted forward along the base of the pyramid as Asad fell back to the remains of the surrounding wall. He placed himself halfway between the pyramid and the colonnaded entrance to the complex.

The sound of gunfire from the north erupted, complementing the occasional mortar shell explosion on the north and western side of the camp. As Buck turned the corner of the pyramid, he could see men rushing in the direction of the attack.

His plan was to stay close to the pyramid and enter the camp between the stone structure and the tents. Once in the center of the camp, he would enter the tent he believed Professor Carter to be in, free him and retreat as quickly as possible. Buck knew he had to make his way past the outer semicircle of tents housing soldiers, pass the communications tent, and he should be there. It was the comm tent that had him worried. He expected that no matter how effective the distraction, both the comm and holding tents would be guarded. He trusted Jock to be on the lookout for anyone coming in behind him as he moved forward.

Buck stayed low and ran for the first line of tents. As luck would have it, a Nazi rushed around the corner of the nearest barrack tent, spotting Buck. The German started to shout when a sniper's bullet struck him in the back, the shock instantly silencing him.

Buck continued forward, behind the first row of barracks and further into the enemy camp. He paused in the shadows of the tent and looked around. No sign that he had been spotted. Buck sprinted forward to the next line of tents, scanning ahead and behind as he went. Next was the communication tent. Buck cautiously moved forward. He stopped behind the communications tent. His ears picked up some activity on the inside, a deep voice thundering out swear words in German, and the cackle of a long-range radio. He realized he knew the deep voice – it was Krause. He seemed to be hurling commands to someone on the radio. Buck risked a moment to listen, always on the look for useful intelligence. As Buck listened, and the possible meaning of the conversation sank in, he thought, 'That's not possible...'

Buck redirected his attention back to the mission at hand. He took a second to gather himself, and then ran to the rear of the next tent. 'This is it,' he told himself. Buck pulled the knife from his belt and cut a slit in the tent. He hesitated, then pushed inside, knife at the ready. If there was any resistance, he wanted to deal with it quietly.

Inside the tent, a man with grey hair and a short beard was tied to a chair in one corner. He looked as if he had been put through the ringer, his gaunt face reflecting the effects of his captivity. A guard armed with a carbine was at the door opposite. Both were looking towards the entrance, their attention was consumed by the noise of the attack outside. Buck quickly attacked the guard from behind, wrapping his left arm around the Nazi's face, pulling him back to meet the point of his knife.

The man in the chair stared at Buck, eyes wide with fear, which was then quickly replaced with hope. Buck put his finger to his lips, warning the Professor to remain quiet. Buck moved behind the old man, and started cutting the ropes that bound him to the chair.

Suddenly several loud explosions sounded from the north. "What is that?" the Professor asked quietly.

"That would be our friends disabling a bunch of Nazi vehicles," Buck whispered. "Can you stand? We need to get out of here fast."

Professor Carter slowly nodded, and slowly stood up. He had to catch himself before he regained his balance. "Where is Katie?"

"Safe – you can see her later. Come with me." Buck grabbed the old man's arm and led him out of the tent through his makeshift back door.

In the few moments Buck had been in the tent, the camp had transformed into a smoky battleground. Gunfire continued to sound behind them as the incoming whistle and explosion of mortars echoed around them. Smoke rolled between the tents as Buck ran, Emmitt Carter close behind him. Buck was impressed with the old man's ability to keep up, especially after his time as a Nazi prisoner.

As they reached the cover of the last tent, Buck stopped and pulled Emmitt down close to the base of the Pyramid. He looked south across the courtyard. A round of phosphorus M2 shells had just hit, and the open area ahead of them was filling with smoke.

Buck pointed to the opposite side of the courtyard, towards the colonnaded entrance. "We need to make a break for that exit point. We are going to go around the corner, head the back side of the courtyard, and then make our way to the exit." He then drew both colts, clicked off the safety, and handed one to Emmitt. "Can you shoot?"

"It's been a while, but yes, I've fired a gun before. I won't swear I'm terribly accurate, though."

"Good. Shoot anyone that looks like one of the Krauts. Don't worry about being accurate; just make anyone coming at you think twice. We'll have help. Our men are going to provide cover fire from both sides. Got it?"

The professor nodded. His face betrayed his bewilderment but he was clearly ready to escape the German's grasp.

Buck slapped him on the back. "Hang in there, you're doing great. Stick with me, and do as I say. OK?" Buck didn't give him time to think or react. He pulled Emmitt with him, running alongside the pyramid to the corner, and then cut sharply to the left to follow the southern edge of the ancient tomb.

Buck expected any pursuit to come from the camp, so he kept Emmitt ahead of him. He was aware of a few shots being fired over his head – Asad was providing cover from the ruined wall as they made for the east side of the courtyard. Buck turned and squeezed off a couple rounds just as they turned towards the exit. Asad's cover fire seemed to be keeping any pursuit back against the far side of the courtyard, but the smoke from the M2 shells had obscured visibility so well he couldn't really tell.

"Lead the way, Asad, I have the rear," Buck said. Asad leapt from behind a half-standing wall and took the point. He led them behind the ruined wall, back towards the colonnade. Emmitt followed only a few yards behind, squeezing of a few rounds for cover. Buck stayed just behind Emmitt, looking for pursuing Germans. The smoke made it nearly impossible.

Within seconds, Asad disappeared into the dark colonnade. He waited for Emmitt to reach his position, where he took the Professor by the arm, guiding Emmitt down the corridor towards the exit. "Stay with me, Professor Carter. Mister Haggard will watch our backs."

Buck paused at the side the colonnade near the entrance, looking back for pursuers, when a shadow violently swooped down from above. Buck felt a sudden blow to his chest, knocking the wind out of him. His pistol flew out of his hand, lost in the smoke of the attack. Buck hit the ground on his back, instinctively rolling to his side, hoping to avoid a second blow. He was still crouched on the ground when he recognized his massive assailant – Wilhelm Krause. 'He jumped me from the top of the colonnade,' Buck thought. 'Sneaky bastard.'

Krause glared as Buck stood up.

"Long time no see," Buck said, taking stock of his position. He was in the open, with Krause between him and the exit.

"I knew you'd come," Krause growled. "You will not keep us from the Stone." His right hand unsnapped his holster cover as he approached Buck.

Buck realized Krause had a serious advantage. With only his knife, he was effectively unarmed. "You know me, Willy. I never miss a good party."

Krause's hand rested on his Mauser. As he spoke, he slowly pulled it from the holster. "This one will be your last... I am going to enjoy – "

A low, deep whistle from above interrupted Krause. Buck, in an instant of realization, turned his head and covered his face.

A brilliant white burst of phosphorous appeared just to the left of Krause, temporarily blinding him. Hot particles of phosphorus settled on his arms and face. Smoke instantly materialized all around the two opponents.

Buck realized Krause had a serious advantage

Buck reacted quickly, lowering his shoulder and charging Krause. He hit him hard, knocking him back towards the impact. Krause hit the ground hard. Buck hesitated, considering his options. He had an old debt to repay Krause, but this wasn't the time. "We're not done," he muttered.

Before Krause could recover, Buck was sprinting down the path between the ancient columns. Within seconds he was out of the door, heading straight for the path he and Asad ascended less than twenty five minutes before.

Chapter 6 - Asad's Compound, Old Cairo - Egypt

Buck woke as the sun broke the horizon, climbing over Old Cairo. The rescuers had regrouped at Asad's fortified compound just a few hours ago. Buck rolled out of his bed, cleaned himself up, dressed in freshly cleaned, weather-beaten linen shirt and khakis and went downstairs. As he reached the first floor, the smell of food and coffee caught his attention. Buck followed the smell to the outdoor patio.

Asad had his butler prepare a lavish breakfast on a large round table in the center of the patio. The food was a mix of local breakfast dishes, consisting of Foul (Fava beans with cumin, salt and pepper, lemon, and olive oil), Large Falafels known as Taamaya, and Beid Bel Basterma (Eggs with dried beef and ghee).

And best of all, Buck saw a large carafe of traditional American coffee. Asad had developed an affinity for American style coffee when he and Buck worked together during the war.

The Carters, Jock, Asad and his men were already seated and helping themselves to generous helpings of the food. Buck took his hat off and seated himself between Jock and the Professor. Asad sat at the head of his table, with Hakeem on his right and Ibrahim on his left side. Kate was next to Ibrahim, then Emmitt, Buck and Jock rounded out the breakfast table. Buck noticed her hair was down, instead of her usual pony tail.

Buck noted that Professor Carter had heaping portions of all three dishes. He appeared to be making up for some lost time from his captivity.

As Buck helped himself to some Foul and Beid bel Basterma, he turned to face Kate and her father. "How are you doing today?" He asked, eyes resting on Kate.

'Good," Kate replied. "And based on Dad's appetite, he's doing well too."

Emmitt took a gulp of black coffee, and sat back. "I am better now. I have to admit, while I like German food, the meals they provided to me were less than desirable. "He looked around the table. "This, however, is quite delicious. Which makes me realize,

I do not yet know who my benefactors are – I'm afraid my baser needs for food got the better of me. Outside of my daughter, I don't really know who I am indebted to."

"That's OK," Buck said. "We didn't really leave time for introductions last night."

Buck motioned towards Asad. "I'll start by introducing our host, Asad Madboury Shadid." Asad humbly bowed his head as Buck continued. "This is his house and his table, and we all benefit from his hospitality.

"To his left is Ibrahim, a Bedouin leader and expert at desert warfare tactics, and to his right is Hakeem from Nubia, one hell of a warrior. I was lucky enough to work with this crew when Germany was occupying North Africa.

"To my left is my partner Jock Howard, and I'm Henry Haggard, but call me Buck. We are the ones your daughter enlisted to help get you to safety, but we all owe Asad and his men for the help they provided last night."

Kate spoke, "I agree, and I can compensate Mr. Shadid, I just hope it is enough."

Asad put his hand up. "Please – do not worry yourself. In this case, my services are free. I am only too happy to strike at the Nazi remnants that still desecrate our country.

"In fact, I think we are not done. I suspect they will be looking to counter, and we need to be prepared to end this."

"Yes, we do need to talk about our next steps," Buck said. "We have a few things to sort out, including how we get the Carters safely away from here, and out of the Nazi's reach for good. However, I suggest we get a good breakfast first."

Emmitt spoke, "Then for now, please accept heartfelt thanks to all of you. I'm very much in your debt. I'm not sure how much longer I could have held up.

"And in the interest of things we need to discuss, let me also say this. It is absolutely critical that these people do not recover the Covenant Stone. "

"Then let us finish our breakfast," Asad replied. "Afterwards, we can meet upstairs, and decide what we are going to do."

As the meal continued, conversation turned to Emmitt's captivity. Jock raised the question after Emmitt had consumed most of his rather large servings. "Professor, would you mind walking us through what happened at the Dead Sea and Petra? We followed clues you left, but I'm just trying to put your part of the story together so I have a complete picture."

Emmitt nodded, "Of course. I think you know I was following up in an earlier dig into the caves south of Qumran. I found the first key about six months ago. I knew there was more, but I wasn't able to get back to Palestine until last month.

"My friend Oren Shanks offered to join me, but I knew that I had been followed from the states. In fact, there were two factions, I guess you would call them, also searching for these objects. Both had visited me in the states. It was clear the Germans had rather nefarious motivations. Subtlety isn't actually their strong suit, you know.

"The other visitor was a man by the name of Aram Avakian."

Jock and Buck exchanged glances at this.

"You've met him?" The Professor asked.

"Yes," Jock said. "In fact, he helped me out of a tough spot in Petra, and he is the one who told us where we could find you."

"I'm not too surprised," Emmitt replied. "At first, I wrote him off as another treasure-hunting mercenary, but I now believe he is an ally. He clearly believes the Covenant Stone must be kept away from the Nazis' at all costs.

"It was Aram that helped me evade the Germans in Palestine. He found me in Jerusalem just I was leaving for the caves. We had met before, so I entertained his request to tag along. In fact, he explained to me that he works with an organization that we may need to talk about. Aram knew that I was being followed by the Nazis, and he offered to help me avoid them.

"Anyway, as we were about to start exploring the cave, we realized that Germans had indeed followed us. I had just uncovered a scroll directing me to the other Key's location, as well as a possible location for the Stone itself, when we heard a commotion below the cave. Mr. Avakian went to dispatch the intruders." Emmitt turned to Buck, "he seemed quite as capable as you seem to be, Mr. Haggard. I suspect he could be a strong ally."

Kate interrupted, "Is that when you scratched the picture of the obelisks below the Paleo-Hebrew script?"

"Yes. After finding the clue to the location of the second key, and seeing proof that the Germans were also after me, I realized that I could not afford to wait to go after it. I knew if anything happened you would follow, and I knew you would remember the trip we took when you were a girl. I took the scroll with me, but wanted to give you a way to follow if possible. I didn't think I could risk sending a message to you using more traditional means.

"Anyway, Mr. Avakian helped me get back to Jerusalem without further incident. Given our close call at the caves, I opted to leave for Jordan right away. I was convinced that I needed to get to the key right away. Aram advised me to wait, and allow him to gather some of his associates to help find the key. Looking back I wish I had listened to him. I insisted that I go right away. He finally agreed, and the plan was for him to meet me in Wadi Musa. I left the same day we got back to Jerusalem while he gathered his men.

"The morning we were to meet, something must have had happened. He was not at our meeting place so I foolishly decided to go to the valley alone. Unfortunately, I was taken prisoner by the Nazis after I got to the top of Jebel Al-Mahdbah. Luckily I had not yet discovered the key.

"After being captured, I quickly realized I needed to misdirect the Germans, or they would likely stumble across the key traipsing all over the top of Mahdbah. I managed to pass the two obelisks off as the next clue, pointing to a location in Egypt. Saqqara seemed a place they would believe simply because of its age. Many of the tombs go back to the earliest dynasty in Egypt, and the Nazis knew this artifact was potentially older than the Egyptians classical civilization. I'm not sure how much longer the

Nazis would have bought into my ruse, so your rescue was truly in the nick of time."

Buck replied, "I'd say you are right. They were clearly patrolling Petra looking for something. Not to mention waiting for us." He sat back, scratching his chin. "What about the scroll you found, didn't it give the Stone's location away? Even if the Nazis can't read it, I would think it's only a matter of time before they bring in someone else who can decipher it?"

"Oh no," Emmitt said. "I knew my trip to Jordan may be risky, so I left the scroll with Aram. It seemed the safer option given what I believe is at stake here. The Nazis are digging in the wrong place, at least for the moment."

Asad asked Emmitt, "Tell us why we should trust this Russian you met. I am not sure you weren't set up by him."

Buck piped in. "I agree. Not saying he isn't an ally, but let's be cautious here. Can we determine what his interest is here, and what do we collectively know about him?" Buck looked to either side, from Jock to Emmitt as he stated the last question.

Jock spoke next. "If he's with the Nazis, he had no reason to do what he did for me. He clearly is handy in a fight – he took Krause down pretty quickly, then told me where we could find the Professor. It was clear that he doesn't want to Nazis to have this Stone. I'm not clear if he wants to prevent us – I mean the Professor - from finding it."

"I can answer that," Emmitt said. "He is part of a very old, little-known order called the Sons of Seth. I doubt any of you have heard of it. In fact, it is an extremely old order that goes back to the beginning of known history.

"The Sons of Seth claims that its origin predates the great Flood, based on the line descending from Adam's third son Seth. Not a lot is said of Seth in the Bible, and I believe he is barely, if at all, directly in the Quran. However, Seth seems to holds a special place in the collective mythology of this part of the world.

"The historian Josephus refers to Seth and his descendants as the inventors of ancient wisdom and protectors of many scientific discoveries and inventions; In other sources, it is said that Adam gave Seth secret teachings that would become the Kabbalah; Zohar called Seth the ancestor of all the 'Righteous Ones'; Islamic tradition says that Seth is the keeper of wisdom of several kinds, such as knowledge of time, prophecy of the future Great Flood, and secrets for communing with God. All of this knowledge is said to be held within two secret pillars that only Seth or his followers are able to access.

"I believe much of this is figurative in nature, but the common thread is that Seth and his descendants, or followers, seem to be considered to be the guardians of secret knowledge. In some cases, they may even be tasked with protecting mankind from the abuse of this knowledge."

Jock shook his head. "Why would a Russian be involved in a group like that? Wouldn't the members of this order be of Middle Eastern or Arab descent?"

"Not necessarily. If we are to believe the Flood stories, which involved Seth's ancestors Noah and his sons, all the ancient texts place the Ark's resting place somewhere between Turkey and Armenia. Remember that the roots of these stories, especially the early ones from Abraham's time or before, describe a migration of people from the North down into the area of Canaan and the surrounding countries. Most people of Semitic ancestry don't realize it, but their roots go back to the area between Turkey and Iran, or Southern Georgia, Armenia and Azerbaijan.

"Aram Avakian is in fact, from Armenia. Which brings me to Aram himself, and why I think he may be worthy of our trust.

"First, his actions strongly suggest he is one of the 'good guys', if you will. The first time I met him, it was in the states. He approached me about sharing my research, and asked me to share what I knew. It was only after he realized I was close to finding both keys that he asked me to curtail my work, and even offered to purchase the rights to it. At no time did he threaten me.

"The second time, in Jerusalem and Qumran, he approached me with a request to act as my partner. He warned me about the Nazis, and it was then he let me know who he represented. He knew I would be familiar with the order, and he implored me to help find the artifacts, but not to go public with them until he could ensure their safety. His primary motivation is to keep the Covenant Stone out of Nazi hands. I've already told you that he kept me out of their hands once.

"Last but not least, he rescued Mr. Howard from the same Germans, and told him where you could find me. He did not have to share that."

"And as a matter of fact," Jock added, "he also told me how we could reach him if we need help again. He seems to have his own purpose or interests, but I agree we are basically on the same side."

Asad looked around the table. "We have quite a bit to talk through today. Let's finish our breakfast and meet upstairs to decide how we will proceed."

Asad and his men, Buck, Jock and the Carters met in Asad's makeshift war room above the patio. As the group took their seats at the table a wiry bearded Arab brought in two large carafes, one with coffee, the other full of water. Buck noticed Kate had her leather satchel, tucked under the table at her feet.

Buck started the conversation while the carafe of coffee was passed around the table. "Let's start with the Germans. There are a few questions I think we need to deal with. In my mind, we have these questions to deal with:

"First, what do we know about their original plans, and how well are they resourced? Professor Carter, I'm hoping you at least overheard or picked something we can use while you held captive.

"Second, what will their reaction be now that we've disrupted their plans - What can we expect them to do next?

"Last, we need to talk a little more about Aram Avakian and his order, the Sons of Seth. That seems like a wild card, and I think we need to understand more about how they fit in."

The Professor spoke up. "I agree, all good questions. However, there is a fourth issue, and we can save it for later. We must talk about the Covenant Stone itself."

Buck took a breath. "Ok, I'll start at the top of the list." He looked around the room. "We know they have a small company of men, about a hundred. They have trucks, jeeps and motorcycles and seem to have a good supply of weapons. I saw no evidence of heavy artillery, it was all light infantry and small arms. The damage we inflicted last night won't really slow them down much.

"They know we aren't going to come back to them at their camp. They are mobile, and probably pissed off. There is no question Krause will want to hit back as hard as he can. I've had a few run-ins with this man, and he is vicious.

"But first, let's talk about what they were doing. That context may help us understand what they are likely to do next. Professor, we know they were trying to get you to reveal this stone to them. What can you tell us about their activities?"

Emmitt Carter shook his head. "I'm not sure I can provide enough information about their plans, but a few things were clear to me from their behavior, especially the leader, Krause.

"First, they knew that the stone would most likely be found in Egypt. They had a supply convoy ready to go before bringing me down from Jordan, that's not something that they needed me to figure out.

"Second, they clearly believe in its supposed power. Even if you believe that is truly just a myth, it will embolden these Nazis to rebuild their movement. Krause is almost fanatical in his belief that the Reich will rise again. And he may be leading this effort locally, but he is answering to someone that he fears. Comments he made during an interrogation made it clear he is under pressure to find this relic soon. He knows it is somehow connected to Egypt, but he is not sure where to look.

"Last, they already clearly have some funding and resources or we wouldn't see a company of nearly a hundred soldiers camped in the desert.

"I should point out that when they brought me here, I misdirected them to Saqqara as a distraction. The scroll I found in Palestine indicated a newer resting place for the Stone, and I wanted to keep them away from the correct location as long as possible. I knew that Katie would follow, and I suspect that Mr. Avakian is not far away.

"Anyway, the increasing intensity of their interrogations made it clear to me that whoever Krause answers to is losing patience. My captors started out with keeping me fed, almost as if they wanted to indoctrinate me by and exerting some emotional pressure on me, but the last week, it was starting to intensify into physical abuse. They have found nothing useful under the Saqqara pyramid, so my ruse had pretty much run its course. I'm not sure I would have lasted more than a day or two longer."

Buck put his hand up, indicating that Emmitt should pause. "I agree that Krause is working for someone else, and that it may be someone with considerable power, at least as far as Nazis go.

"I actually picked up a piece of conversation as I snuck past the comm tent last night. It seems to dovetail with some comments Krause made in front of Jock two days ago. What I overheard has me convinced this Nazi remnant is part of something larger."

Asad focused his eyes on Buck. "Please go on, Mr. Haggard. You are clearly building up to something."

Buck took a deep breath. "Most of you know that before Jock and I left the OSS, we were assigned to investigate the 'Rat Lines' or escape routes from Germany into other countries. What most don't know is just how effective those escape routes were. Some leaders in our government were convinced that most of Hitler's inner circle, possibly including Adolf himself, made it out of Germany alive."

"But the Russians found his body!" said Professor Carter.

"So they say. But we had briefings to the contrary, that the Russian story was propaganda to ease the fears of the public. Britain and the US adopted it. The Allies were anxious to provide a clear, satisfying ending to the Axis threat. You can't do that if any of the Nazi leadership might be alive and running free.

"In fact, Jock and I found quite a bit of evidence that many of his associates did escape to South America, including ones as notorious as Joseph Mengele. We found some evidence of a stronghold protecting someone called 'Herr Wolf' in Argentina. We were never able to move on it though."

"Who exactly is the Herr Wolf? I've heard that name at least twice since we met in Quito." Kate asked.

Jock answered her. "We don't really know, but we do know this about that name. In his early days Hitler referred to himself as Herr Wolf. When he met Eva Braun, Hitler introduced himself as Herr Wolf, and he referred to his SS as 'his pack of wolves'.

"He even changed his sister's name to Frau Wolf. And last but not least, the name Adolf is a derivative of Athalwolf, meaning Nobel Wolf." Jock looked to Buck as he finished.

Buck took the cue. "Most likely, some new leader in the Party took Herr Wolf as a call sign to 'honor' Hitler. If I am right, Krause is answering to someone connected to that inner circle."

"At any rate, whether these ratzis are led by the ghost of Adolf himself or one of his right-hand men, they are on a mission, they are well funded and motivated, and they will not stop until this comes to a clear conclusion.

"It's not enough just to get the Carters back to the States. We need to find a way to end this."

Asad shook his head as his servant refilled his water glass. "I agree that you are right, Buck. But we no longer hold any advantage by being able to launch a surprise attack. I don't have enough men to hold out, much less defeat a company."

Professor Carter raised his hand to get the room's attention. "I need to speak," he said.

Everyone in the room turned to Emmitt.

"During breakfast, I already said that the Nazis, or at least their leaders, do seem to believe in the power of the Covenant Stone. At the very minimum, it motives them just as Mr. Haggard says, and that alone is very dangerous.

"In the course of my studies, I have found reason to believe they may even be right. Whether you believe the Bible or Quran are purely theological, myth-based literary works or truly reflections of history, I can say this for certain; All supposed 'myths' have a basis in fact. This object is not just a fantasy, and it is almost certainly not without some power that I cannot explain. The obelisk keystones alone are evidence that we are dealing with something we do not understand."

Asad tapped the table, causing Emmitt to pause. "But from what I have heard, they are only crystalline stones. How does that suggest we are dealing with some otherworldly power? The existence of a temple does not prove the existence of a god – we see that all over Egypt. That is why the ancient gods of Egypt gave way to Allah. "

"True," the Professor replied. "Those temples we see all over Egypt show no evidence of anything but a complex mythology. Their only power is in what they can teach us about the classic Egyptian civilization we are all aware of.

"But the keys are different." Emmitt turned to his daughter. "Did you bring them?" he asked.

Kate produced her brown leather satchel. She placed it on the table beside her father. Emmitt opened it and produced the wooden box containing the first key. He set the box on the table, then reached back into the satchel, removing a bundle of rags, slightly smaller than the box.

Emmitt opened the box. "This is the first key, the one I found in Palestine. When I discovered it, I immediately noticed something strange about it." He looked up at the old Arab servant. "Can we close the blinds and dim the lights, please?"

As the old man dimmed the electric lights and pulled the window shade closed, Emmitt continued. "This was very noticeable in the Qumran cave, since I had very little light, I think you will see it well enough here. "

The keystone was casting a faint blue-white light on the table. Asad and his two lieutenants stared in amazement.

"As you can see, this crystalline carving gives off its own light. There is no explanation I can offer, this is not the fluorescent moonstone that is mined here, this is clear crystal. It is also not dependent upon an outside source of light to 'charge' it as we would expect with a fluorescent object."

"Then where does it get the energy from?" Asad asked.

"I'm not sure," Emmitt replied. "But look here. I wasn't aware of this until I got back here, and my daughter filled me in on her adventure in Petra." He proceeded to slowly unwrap the bundle of rags, revealing the crystalline key from Jebel Al-Mahdbah. It produced the same eerie glow as he held it in his hands.

Emmitt then set the two objects about a foot apart, in the middle of the table. The two objects seemed to react to each other, the glow increasing in intensity until the room was nearly as bright as if the lights were on.

Everyone at the table looked on in awe. Emmitt spoke up. "There is no external power source, and these objects react to each other. They clearly produce some sort of energy. It is not entirely stable either. If one were to handle either of these objects carelessly, you might find yourself unconscious on the floor." Emmitt glanced at Buck with a wry smile. "In fact, both Buck and I have experienced this first hand.

"You will notice that this energy intensifies as these objects are brought near each other. They seem to amplify each other's energy. I don't know if this is a supernatural phenomenon or some new natural element we have never seen before.

"If these are the keys to unlock the hiding place of the Covenant Stone, and they clearly have some energy-producing properties we have never seen before. As I said earlier, the keys are different from anything we have found in any archeological expedition. For this reason alone, it stands to reason that the Stone itself is also at least as powerful.

"The texts I discovered in some of my Sumerian and Babylonian digs tell us the Covenant Stone holds power that was used to build great structures; Massive structures like the Tower of Babel, which was supposed to reach the heavens; that the

Stone was also used to shape Eden, before Man was expelled; and that the abuse of its power has always led to tragedy.

"I don't know how these objects were actually used, but it's clear to me that this alleged 'myth' is based in some sort of historical truth. We can't risk allowing a remnant of the Nazi Party to gain access to something like this. Even if there is only a remote chance of it having some undiscovered, powerful properties like the ones described in the ancient texts.

"Securing this Stone and protecting it from Nazi designs must be our priority. Even if these people are only a small remnant of that evil, they cannot be allowed to have it. I truly believe the risk is far too great."

Asad nodded. "Clearly we are dealing with something otherworldly, perhaps Godly." He said. "But to protect it from the Nazis, we must know where it is. Have you been able to determine that?"

Emmitt turned to Kate. "I may have mentioned earlier that the scroll I found in the cave, the one I left with Aram Avakian, indicated the location of the Covenant Stone. It is here in Egypt, and in fact it is close by.

"There have long been rumors of an underground complex beneath the Sphinx, called the Hall of Records. This is largely considered to only be a rumor, but the scroll I found suggested it is at least based on some actual underground chambers beneath the Sphinx. The Stone was hidden there, in a place referred to as the Osiris Tomb.

"Osiris is commonly known as the leader of the Egyptian pantheon, and a lot of mythology has been built up around that idea. However, some archeologists have theorized he was based on an actual living person, from before the known first dynasty rulers. If that is true, this may be the tomb of the person who was greatly revered, possibly for founding what would become the Egyptian civilization!

"Keep in mind that all of that is conjecture, but it fits with my theory that some ancient knowledge was used to "kick-start" the massive growth we see in ancient Egypt, as well as in other places around the world.

"Anyway, the scroll we found was written around five or six hundred BC, so it's a relatively recent document. It did not provide any history of the Stone, so tracing its provenance wasn't possible. It only speaks of the Stone's power, and that fact that it was lost for centuries, then declares the Stone's current resting place in a tomb under the Sphinx. It doesn't go into how it got there, or why, so this is not a certain thing. But it is all we have, and I think it's enough to at least attempt recovery."

The Arab spy slipped quietly from the room as Emmitt closed his speech. He ran downstairs and outside. As he exited the compound, and lost himself in the Cairo foot traffic, he congratulated himself on how easy it had been to infiltrate and pose as a house servant. His German employers would pay well for this information.

Jock heard a small metal-on-metal squeak behind him. He turned just as the Arab servant slipped out and quietly shut the door. 'That's odd' he thought. Jock stood and slowly opened the door and looked out. He tried to shake an uneasy feeling as he looked both ways down the hallway. The Arab was not in sight.

Jock stepped back into the War Room, and observed the water and coffee carafes were nearly half full.

Asad was asking about the next course of action as Jock interrupted. "How long has that servant worked here?"

Asad, seemingly irritated, responded, "Why? Has he done something?"

"Yes, he's disappeared. And he didn't go to get more water or coffee, there is plenty left here." Jock paused, looking around the table. "I have a bad feeling about this."

Asad paused. "Now that you mention it, I do not know. My butler hires help as we need it, so I don't often get to know all the people who work here." Asad turned to Hakeem, and said, "Check it out." Hakeem silently acknowledged the order, quickly exiting the room.

Buck watched Emmitt carefully repack the keystones. He seemed lost in thought as he considered what was likely to happen next. After a moment he stood up. "I'll go in after the Stone. We can't send a platoon of men into the tunnels under the Sphinx, and we have to assume the Nazis will come after us, for the Keys, and then the Stone.

"This has to be a small group, one or two of us that go to recover the artifact. What we will need to plan for is the possibility of the Nazis coming after us while I'm in there. We will need an exit strategy, and that probably means a pretty intense fight."

Asad looked at Ibrahim. "What are your thoughts? Can we stand against the Germans long enough for Mr. Haggard to recover the Stone?"

Ibrahim thought a moment, and finally shook his head. "Not in an open fight. They are too many – this is not a desert ambush, and we do not have surprise on our side this time. We will need more men to truly stand up to them."

Kate shook her head, visibly frustrated. "My father held out against their interrogations for weeks. We have to finish this or everything we've done so far has been for nothing!"

Asad agreed, his expression showing compassion for her plea. "Yes I know -"

He stopped as Hakeem came back into the room. "The servant is gone. I asked some of the other staff, and no one seemed to recognize him, including your butler. He is not one of the staff."

Jock said, "I was afraid of that. I think we need to assume we have been infiltrated." He paused, head down in thought. "Maybe it's a good thing he left when he did." Jock turned to

Asad. "We have an option we haven't really explored yet. Maybe it can help tip the odds in our favor."

Emmitt made the same connection. "The Sons of Seth."

Jock continued, "Yes. Before Avakian and I parted, he agreed we may need to help each other again. In fact, I suspect he is nearby. He warned us to rescue you before something - he didn't say what - happens. His comments gave me the distinct impression that the Sons of Seth have some sort of plans to attack the Nazis anyway.

Jock looked at Buck as he continued, "You know what they say about the 'enemy of my enemy'. At any rate, Aram gave me a call sign and a radio frequency to try to reach him. It's worth a try."

Asad looked doubtful. "Can we trust him?"

"If we are serious about ending this, we may have no choice," Buck said. "As it stands now, we are outnumbered almost three to one. It's a long shot, but I think we have to try." He turned to Jock, "See if you can reach Avakian as soon as we wrap this up." Jock nodded in acknowledgment.

Emmitt interjected, "Yes, we do need them. But we also need to think about how we prepare you to go after the Stone. You can't go into the chambers beneath the Sphinx alone. Someone with knowledge of this regions ancient languages is likely critical to your success. It is unlikely the Stone is sitting in plain sight. I should go too."

"No!" Kate said. "I'll go. You've risked enough."

Emmitt stood up, as if to emphasize his disagreement. "Katie, I have to. I know what to look for, and in many ways, I started this through my research. I have to see it to the end."

"Dad, I've studied the Egyptian language, and you know I'm better at the other written languages of the Middle East than you are. Besides that, you really haven't recovered from your captivity. You can talk me through any other visual clues or signs I need to look for."

"It's too dangerous, Katie." Emmitt said, shaking his head. "I have to go."

"Professor Carter," Buck interrupted. "I understand why you feel responsible, but you shouldn't carry that burden. The Nazis would be after the Stone whether it was you or someone else who discovered its existence. As far as who goes with me, I've never been the type to bring a woman into a dangerous situation without good reason." Kate shot Buck a defiant look.

Buck continued, "In this case, I have to agree with your daughter. The stakes are high, and you aren't quite ready to go into this situation. I've learned that Kate is pretty resourceful, and besides, we've been through this twice before. I think she can handle this." Kate's defiance gave way to a look of grim satisfaction.

Emmitt sat down, conceding his argument. "You had better take good care of her, Mr. Haggard. She's all I care about in this world."

Buck nodded, and made eye contact with Emmitt. "If I have to, I'll give my life to keep her safe."

Wilhelm Krause stepped out of the medic's tent. The stepped pyramid behind him still had the camp cast in morning shadow. In spite of the burns on the left side of his face and arm, he was thankful to finally be moving around. Now that medic's pain medication was finally kicking in, Krause had a job to do.

Most of the burns were superficial, but some scarring was inevitable. The faint scar on his left cheek, a childhood gift from his father, would be replaced with more obvious damage from the burns. This was one more thing Krause had to hold against Henry James Haggard.

Krause forced himself to stride to his makeshift command center. He had called for a strategy meeting with his two lieutenants, Dieter Schenk and Karl Weiss. He entered the tent and the men inside snapped to attention. German SS and Officer Formalities were still observed in his presence. Krause motioned for them to relax, when he realized a thin, wiry Arab was seated at his command table.

Dieter and Karl sat on either side of the Egyptian, who was visibly nervous. Krause slowly moved to the opposite side of the table and took a seat, his eyes locked on the man. Krause recognized him as one of their Bedouin workers, hired to clear the tunnels around the Step Pyramid. The man was staring nervously at Krause's burns.

"Is this the man that followed Haggard?" he asked.

Karl spoke. "This is Ammon, the one who agreed to follow the American and his allies. He was able to sneak into their base of operations disguised as a servant. He says he has information you will want to hear."

Krause focused his gaze on Ammon. "Let's hear it."

The Egyptian shook his head, he was nervous, but he was also ready to bargain. "I want payment first," he stated in fluent English. "My price is – "

Krause pulled his Mauser out and sat it on the table in front of him. He smiled and calmly stated, "No, I want to know it's worth paying for first. If it is, I'll pay you well. If it's not, you will be lucky to leave with your life." Krause liked the man's spirit, but was in no mood to negotiate.

Ammon hesitated. He instantly saw that he was not going to negotiate a higher price for this information. 'Best to disclose and take what I can get', Ammon thought. He found himself speaking in a hurried fashion.

"The American is meeting with a known gangster, Asad Madboury. Asad's men are known to be fearsome fighters. All of them fought the Germans in the War. They are looking for a hidden tomb called the Osiris Tomb."

"Where?" Krause asked. His tone was cold.

"North of here. They believe they will find it under the Great Sphinx, and they plan on doing it tonight."

Krause smiled. "Pay the man his price and get him out of here. We are going to engage Captain Haggard's friends and take the Stone from their cold dead hands."

Chapter 7 - Temple of the Sphinx, Giza Plateau - Egypt

Buck parked the old jeep at the East side of the Giza Plateau. Kate sat in the passenger seat, her hair now pulled back into her usual pony tail. Her appearance gave the impression that she was all business. Buck forced himself to look at the scene ahead of them. As Kate reviewed her journal, Buck took in the view to the west.

The late afternoon sun was about to set down on the scene around them. Behind lay the village of Nazlet El-Samman, on the outskirts of Cairo. To the front stood the three Great Pyramids, forming an ancient, man-made horizon that would soon eclipse the solar disc above. Immediately in front of the center pyramid stood the Funeral temple of Khafre, from which extended an ancient causeway recently exposed by archeologists. From his vantage point, the causeway was partially obscured by a great monument. A heavily weathered stone head sat atop the Body of a lion – The Great Sphinx. Two hundred and forty feet long and sixty-six feet high, the body of the statue sat in a depression, essentially carved from the floor of the Giza Plateau. The head and shoulders still towered above the desert floor. The causeway proceeded in a straight line from Khafre's Pyramid and temple, passing by the south side of the Sphinx, terminating at a field of Jumbled walls and columns that extended from Buck's far left across the front of the Sphinx.

As Buck appreciated the incredible age and extent of the history in front of him, he found his mind drifting back to an event after the meeting with Asad's men.

After some additional discussion, it was agreed that Buck and Kate would search for the entrance to the underground temple. Asad would post lookouts on the north side of the Sphinx temple ruins in case Buck and Kate ran into trouble, as well as to the

South, looking for the inevitable German incursion. The rest of his men were to take up positions along the outskirts of the local village, where they would wait.

Ibrahim would act as the Southern lookout, as well as keep a small contingent of men ready to attempt to slow Krause and his company down. Hakeem would command the north lookouts and hidden fighters. Asad would tail Buck and intervene as necessary. All would maintain radio contact to coordinate defensive actions between lookouts and fighting forces. Their goal was to defend Buck and Kate's search while Jock attempted to contact Aram Avakian and bring help.

When Buck exited the War Room, Kate followed. As they started to walk down the stairs to the main floor, Buck stopped and turned to face her. "Are you sure you're up for this? It could be as dangerous as Petra – maybe more so."

Kate looked determined. "I am. I want to thank you for backing me up in there. I know Dad just sees his little girl in danger, and I'm not sure how the others perceive me. Anyway, I have to do this."

Buck nodded and started to turn when Kate added, "There is more to you than I thought, Mr. Haggard – I mean Buck."

"How so? I'm just doing what I was hired to do."

"No, you're not," Kate interjected. "You were hired to find Dad and get him to safety, and you've done that. What we are doing next is bigger than anything we planned on back in Quito, and we all know you aren't obligated to go that far.

"You're not some mercenary. You're a good man, and I'm glad you're here." With that, Kate stood on her toes and kissed Buck on the cheek.

He turned his head in surprise, bringing them eye to eye. Kate kept eye contact with him as she squeezed his arm. Just for a moment, Buck thought they were going to share an even more intimate moment when Jock walked up, speaking loudly. "We don't have access to com equipment here. I'll head over to the Goose and try the ARC-5 radio to reach Avakian."

Buck and Kate turned to face Jock as they stepped apart. Kate looked back at Buck. "I'll see you outside by the jeep."

She turned away and quickly descended the stairs. Jock looked at Buck, a puzzled expression on his face. "Did I just interrupt something?"

Buck's attention returned to the present as Kate pointed to the ruins. "These ruins are the remains of the temple dedicated to the Sphinx."

Buck listened as he pulled his lucky Cincinnati Reds cap out of his back pocket, seating it firmly on his head. Kate continued. "Since the Hall of Records is supposed to be under the Sphinx, Dad believes the front door has to be in or around the Sphinx temple. That's the area where we want to focus our search."

Buck half smiled and touched the bill of his cap in acknowledgement. "Lead the way, Ms. Carter." Kate rolled her eyes.

They exited the jeep and picked up their supplies from the back seat. Kate took her brown leather satchel, outfitted with a shoulder strap and containing a flashlight, rope, and the two obelisk-shaped crystal keystones. The keys were wrapped individually to minimize the chance of any reaction while moving about the ruins. She also had the Webley revolver strapped to her hip.

Buck had his remaining colt holstered on his right leg. His Ranger Repeater was hung across his back. He carried spare twelve-gauge cartridge carriers attached the bandolier across his chest. On his left shoulder he carried his own utility bag, with a battery powered lantern, his Army-issue flashlight, matches, a pry bar, and rope.

As they walked towards the ruined temple walls, Kate went over information that her father had shared with her earlier. "These ruins are really two separate temples, built at different times. The newer portion, along with the causeway to the second

Pyramid was added later in preparation for the Pharaoh Khafre's passage into the afterlife." Kate pointed towards the Sphinx and the crumbled walls in front of it. "The older temple, the one dedicated to the Sphinx itself, sits directly in front.

Kate took the lead into the ruins. The two spent the next twenty minutes walking through the remains of the temple, looking for anything that resembled a sealed door or tunnel entrance. As they searched, Kate continued with another of her history lessons. "Archeologists traditionally think the Sphinx and this temple date from the time of Khafre, who also built the temple next door. A very few believe the Sphinx predates Khafre, perhaps by thousands of years, but we have no verifiable proof.

"The belief that an underground system of tunnels and possibly a repository of ancient knowledge has roots in antiquity. Pliny wrote of a tomb and passages. Later, after the crusades, the Rosicrucian order claimed that a temple with a great library and possibly a tomb were under the Sphinx, and that a series of passages connect it with all of the Pyramids.

"Both views consider the Sphinx to predate the old Kingdom – possibly by thousands of years. In recent decades, crank psychics have latched onto and popularized this idea, and frankly have driven any reputable scientists away from considering the notion of an older civilization underneath the classic Egyptian society we know of."

"But you don't feel that way," Buck observed. "Why not?"

"Besides Pliny and the Rosicrucian documents? I know of two modern accounts from respected archeologists that support these stories. In 1914, Professor George Reisner from Harvard claimed to have discovered passages and rooms that extended from inside the head of the Sphinx down to a temple underneath. In addition, just prior to the war, Dr. Salim Hassan, an Egyptian Archeologist from the University of Cairo, privately published an article in the UK that described his discovery of a temple and passage complex beneath the Sphinx.

"Both men intended to return to explore these discoveries, but in both cases, the wars over the last few decades prevented them from following through."

"Why haven't others followed in their footsteps? Surely there are plenty of eager historians that want to make a name for themselves."

"Most likely because of the inherent instability in the political situation here. Besides that, both articles were published in private institutions seriously limited exposure to the general public. Only people like my father, with access to those institutions have any access to the actual articles. This information just isn't that well known."

"Did either one happen to document how they made their way into these chambers?" Buck asked.

"Not really, they were really very cautious with what was shared. Neither account was really clear about the specifics. Dad just assumed the most likely entrance was in or near the temple ruins."

"OK," Buck said. "Unfortunately, I'm not seeing any indications of a passage or tunnel entrance inside the ruins. Let's get a closer look at the Sphinx.

"I've led several trips into the Amazon, and once in a while someone actually finds an old temple or building buried in the jungle. One thing I learned is that older structures rarely have a working front door. Something to keep an eye out for might be a ventilation shaft or some sort of secondary access designed for light or air circulation. We got lucky in Palestine and Petra. Now it might be more productive to look for something like that."

"Great idea, Buck," Kate said. She shot him a smile. "There's hope for you yet."

Kate led the way from the temple ruins down into the low area in front of the statue. Between the six-foot high paws sat a square stone pedestal about three feet high. Further back, where the long forelegs met the body, a large stone stele with hieroglyphic writing stood.

"What's on the stele?" Buck asked. "Anything that could help us?"

"I'm not sure, but I doubt it. The tablet tells the story of how Thutmose was granted kingship and power over Egypt. As a prince, he was working nearby and came here to rest. In a midday dream, Ra spoke to him and granted his kingship over the land."

"OK, let's look around." The two adventurers walked clockwise around the Sphinx. As they walked the length of the body, they observed two stone boxes or pedestals built into the sides at intervals. Buck noticed that large portions of the body were heavily eroded. Some of it seemed like extreme damage compared to other ancient buildings or monuments in the area.

"How is it the body is so heavily eroded?" Buck asked. "I see damage to the head, but it doesn't seem very consistent in nature."

Kate shook her head. "Who really knows? There is some trace evidence this is much older than classical Egyptian history, but that's generally considered to be sort of a 'fringe' theory. Some claim it is much older, and that the old or middle kingdom rulers modified it to suit their needs. You see the erosion marks on the Sphinx body – some of that looks like water, possibly flood, damage. But in this environment, it's hard to prove that.

"What I find interesting is that the Sphinx spent hundreds, if not thousands of years buried up to the head in sand. You would expect that would minimize the weathering. But where you see the brick and mortar sections missing, the underlying body looks far more damaged, as if by either wind, water, or both.

"It's also clear the head is distinctly classical Egyptian, especially with the headdress. Some argue that this is a modification to the original structure. But again, that's impossible to prove."

Buck looked, studying the sides of the Sphinx's' body. There were deep grooves cut into the underlying stone, looking very much like water damage to his eyes. "Maybe we'll find out, if we can find a way into this thing."

Further examination failed to reveal anything useful, so Kate led the way further back.

At the rear, Kate pointed out a small opening at ground level, a recess about a foot high that went back into the statue's body. Buck knelt and started digging sand away, enlarging the hole. A feeling of anticipation swelled as he pulled out his light and pointed it down into the recess. He was immediately disappointed. "Looks like a dead end," he said.

"Buck, if I didn't know better, you almost looked excited. Come on, let's keep looking."

Buck took the lead as they made their way back around towards the front. He observed two more box-like pedestals at slightly different intervals along the north side of the body, and similar water or wind damage to the body, but no clear signs of an air vent or access shaft.

They came back around to the front, stopping in front of the massive paws of the Great Sphinx.

Buck looked around, eventually focusing on the raised pedestal. "This looks familiar, doesn't it?"

Kate turned her head. "It does remind me of the pedestal in the cave in Petra..."

Buck motioned towards the Stele between the Sphinx's legs. "Humor me... Can you translate that?"

Kate walked back to the Stele and ran her hands over the ancient text. She looked at the worn stone inscriptions. "A lot of the first part is really just exposition that talks about how great the god Ra-Atum is, and how Thutmoses IV is a beloved leader. Further down the stele, we get into the actual story. Here the text reads:

"'Behold thou me, my son, Thutmose. I am thy father, Ra-Atum; I will give to thee my Kingdom upon earth at the head of the living. Thou shalt wear the White Crown and the Red Crown upon the Throne of Geb, the Hereditary Prince. The land shall be thine, in its length and in its breath, that which the eye of the All-Lord shines upon. The food of the Two Lands shall be thine, the great tribute of all countries, the duration of a long period of* *years. My face is directed to you, my heart is to you; Thou shalt be to me the protector of my affairs, because I am ailing in all my limbs. The sands of the Sanctuary, upon which I am, have reached me; turn to me in order to do what I desire. I know that thou art my son, my protector; behold; I am with thee, I am thy leader.*

'*When he finished this speech, the King's Son awoke, hearing this..., he understood the words of Ra-Atum.*'

"The idea is that this stele commemorates where Thutmose fell asleep and had his dream about meeting Ra, who appoints him as his representative on earth. The rest talks about how Thutmoses becomes a great King over all Egypt, with guidance from the god Ra."

Buck was lost in thought. He mumbled to himself, "That almost sounds like a 'Burning Bush' moment." He turned to Kate. "Stories like this usually have some real basis or foundation. What if it wasn't a dream? What if he found some way into the temple, and either the contents or knowledge stored in that temple helped him become this 'great king'?"

Buck walked around the pedestal, intently studying it. His thoughts drifted back to Petra, in the cave where the second Keystone was. It has to have a purpose. There was a faint square depression in the surface. "Let me see the Keys."

Kate unbundled both of the crystal obelisks and handed them to Buck. He gingerly held one in each hand, and facing the Sphinx, slowly brought them together, back to back. They emitted a noticeable glow even in the afternoon sun.

As he held them together, Buck lowered them to the top of the pedestal, aligning the base with the square etched on the surface. The Keystones fit snugly into the depression as if they were a single object. The dim glow from the crystal keystones increased slightly as they made contact with the surface of the pedestal, and then faded. Buck thought he could detect a faint vibration under his feet. A few seconds later, the sound of stone grinding on stone materialized just behind Buck.

He looked up at Kate. Their eyes met in surprise. Both explorers turned to face the sound. Just to the front of the

Sphinx's paws, sand was dropping into a growing void. Beneath the sand, a stone platform dropped several inches and slid to one side, revealing a dark chamber beneath their feet. A rush of stale air erupted from it. Buck walked to the other side of the void, facing towards the Sphinx. It was square, about ten feet by ten feet. Inside he saw a steep stairwell cut into the bedrock. The steps led down into darkness, towards the great statue. Buck's expression gave away his surprise. "Holy mackerel. I really didn't expect *that* to happen."

A stone platform slid to one side, revealing a dark chamber beneath their feet

The slab stopped moving as Kate picked up the obelisk keys and put them away. She walked around to stand beside Buck. He had his light ready, pointing down into the darkness. Buck and Kate exchanged glances, both understanding that this was the end game. They started their descent, side by side.

Asad sat in a battered truck just outside the outskirts of Nazlet El-Samman. His vantage point overlooked the temple ruins that Buck and Kate were exploring. The gathering dusk cast long shadows over the sand as he listened intently to the handheld radio next to him. He quietly hoped that Hakeem's lookout on the north side had spotted something.

Buck and the girl were in the ruins and out of Asad's sight for at least forty-five minutes when his radio cackled to life. It was Hakeem's lookout reporting that Buck and Kate were still walking around the perimeter of the Sphinx. Asad started to acknowledge when a second message came through. "Sir, they just disappeared into the ground."

Asad activated his mic. "Repeat, Khalid. They disappeared?"

"Yes, they somehow opened a door in the ground in front of the Great Sphinx. They appear to have descended into the ground."

Asad paused. 'So they found a way in,' He thought.

"Sir there is more."

"Yes, Khalid?"

"The door in the ground has closed behind them. They appear to be trapped."

Asad put his mic down and looked over the front of his truck, towards the ruins. As he considered ordering his scout to head into the ruins to investigate, another radio transmission came in. It was one of his lieutenants guarding the southern approach to the ruins.

'Captain Asad, this is Ibrahim. We have sighted a convoy of heavy trucks coming over the desert from the south."

"How many?"

Ibrahim replied, "I counted fifteen vehicles, ranging from jeeps to troop trucks. Enough to carry the entire company of Nazi dogs. They will be here within minutes."

"Then it is time to get into position. You know what to do." Asad replied. He had expected this, but had hoped for more time. Buck and the girl were on their own. He now hoped and prayed to Allah that Jock would be successful in bringing help.

On the west side of Cairo, Jock and Emmitt sat in an open air restaurant in a small souq. Aram Avakian sat across from them. Immediately after the meeting in Asad's War Room had ended, Jock was able to contact Aram Avakian on the Goose's ARC-5 radio. Avakian had already guessed that they needed their help, but he had a price, and wanted to talk in person. Jock agreed and arranged for a face-to-face meeting in the marketplace.

"I understand you two need help again," Aram said with a serious tone. He then added, "Mr. Carter, I am glad to see you are safe."

Jock interrupted, "I'm sorry, Mr. Avakian, but we have no time for small talk. I already owe you a debt, and unfortunately we do need your help again. On the other hand, this may work to your benefit, so I'll cut to the chase; I assume you also want the Stone?"

Aram shook his head. "We don't want it. Unfortunately, we can't allow anyone else to have it. The Stone must stay hidden. If it is brought forward into the world, it could be used in terrible ways.

"If you are asking about my price for helping you, it is that we must ensure the Stone remains hidden. From everyone."

Aram turned his attention to Emmitt. "I know that is not the outcome you originally sought, Mr. Carter. But it's important to understand the power that the Stone wields. We crude human beings are not ready for it yet. And keeping the stone hidden also implies that its hiding place, the Hall of Records, must remain secret. It cannot come to light either."

Emmitt sighed, and replied. "I think I do understand. Ultimately, for me it is far more important that we stop this Nazi remnant, and keep my daughter safe. You'll get no argument from me."

Aram nodded. "Then perhaps we can help you."

As Buck and Kate reached the bottom of the steps, the stone slab slid shut above them, cutting off the fading daylight. "Hold my flashlight," Buck said. Kate took the light as Buck pulled out his battery powered lantern and switched it on. As he held it up, it cast a light in a circle around them. They could see the plain stone walls on either side, leading from the steps. The ceiling was well above them. Buck judged that they were at least thirty feet below ground. The corridor ahead sloped downward at about a 20 degree decline. Every few feet, the floor had a drop of about a foot and half, like large steps.

As the corridor sloped away, it also widened to nearly twenty feet. About thirty-five or forty feet ahead, the path ended in a wall that extended to the ceiling above. Buck could just make out a dark opening in the far wall.

"Looks like a door up ahead. Watch your step," he said. Habit forced him to unsnap the holster to his colt.

Kate pointed the flashlight towards the dark opening. It was eight feet wide and at least fifteen feet tall. Two large ornamental cyclopean columns framed the doorway. "Yes," she said quietly. "I will."

Kate used her flashlight to scan the walls to either side as they walked forward. Large square-cut stones formed the walls, with no evidence of plaster overlaying the seams. They were devoid of any hieroglyphic writing or decorative illustrations. The columns that framed the door curved inward over the opening, forming an arch, the only obvious decorative element in the corridor.

Once at the threshold of the door, she said "This architecture doesn't look like Old Kingdom or even the Pre-Dynastic styles. It must be older. I've never seen or read of anything quite like this in Egypt."

"I guess we might prove that 'fringe' theory after all. How old do you think it is?"

"I have no idea. If it's pre-dynastic, we are looking at five, maybe even six thousand years old. If Dad's research is relevant, it might be older. This could change history as we know it."

"Yeah. As much as that intrigues me, we'd better stay focused on our objective first. History lessons can come later."

Buck held the lantern up in an attempt to cast the light as far as possible, and stepped through the large doorway.

The chamber beyond was much larger. The walls extended into the darkness in both directions. Buck had the sense of an even greater expanse ahead. At the limit of his lanterns light, he could just barely make out two rows of large columns extending ahead of them in the darkness.

Buck looked to his left and right before proceeding. About shoulder height a trough filled with a dark substance ran along the walls. Buck dipped his index finger in it, them smelled it and touched it to his tongue.

"Looks like tar residue – it's still oily, not completely dried out." Buck reached into his utility bag and found the matches. "Stand back – this is a little risky, but we need to be able to see."

Kate moved back into the corridor as Buck lit the match. He dropped it into the trough to his left and stepped back into the frame of the doorway. The oily substance sputtered, and then ignited. A flame leapt up and traveled down the length of the trough. The lighted trough ascended sharply until it was twenty five feet off the floor, hit a corner and turned ninety degrees. From the corner the flame continued to spread down the trough, running parallel to the floor around the room.

As Buck and Kate stepped forward, the moving flame picked up speed as it followed the trough around the room. It cast a growing light, revealing the expanse of the large chamber ahead of them. They stood at one end of a large room, close to fifty feet wide and nearly a hundred long. The arched ceiling stretched about forty feet above. Two rows of three massive columns were evenly spaced down the length of the room.

The left and right walls were without decoration, but had tall recesses at regular intervals, ten on each side. The recesses contained shelves filled with various objects; vessels, scrolls, tablets, hundreds of artifacts. The far end of the chamber appeared to end in another massive door, similar in size to the entrance.

As the flame came back around to their right, Buck saw a small open doorway, just six feet by three, in the corner next to them. He walked over to it and directed his light into the shadows beyond. A narrow staircase led up. Buck stepped back away from the smaller door and looked up. Above the burning trough, along the walls on either side, were openings like dark windows into rooms above them. Buck assumed that was most likely where the staircase led. He walked back towards the entrance as Kate went to look at the nearest of the recesses. She motioned Buck over. "These jars, scrolls, tablets – This is the Hall of Records. It's real."

Buck touched her shoulder. "Let's keep looking for the Stone. We'll have time for this stuff later."

They stepped back towards the middle of the room, looking past the cyclopean columns. "That's where I think we should start," Buck said, pointing at the large door on the far end.

As they walked forward, Kate took in as much as she could, directing her flashlight into each of the recessed areas, illuminating ancient texts and documents, knowledge stored for thousands of years. She fought the urge to explore the ancient archives, telling herself she would bring her father back here soon enough.

The second large door was also framed by similar columns, forming another large archway. Two large wooden doors blocked access to the next room. The doors were devoid of markings, except for one decorative metallic plate. Buck was not sure about the material, but it looked like ancient bronze. The seam between the doors split the plate down the center, about five feet off the floor. It was a round, about 18 inches in diameter with a trapezoidal emblem in the center. The trapezoid was 10 inches tall, narrow at the top and wide at the bottom, symmetrical on both sides.

Buck pushed on one door, then the other. Both refused to move. He stepped back looking for a release. Kate pointed to the circle. "What does that remind you of?" she asked.

"Of course – Let's try one of the keys again."

Kate took one out and unwrapped it. She carefully placed it against the trapezoid on the doors, and once again the faint glow of the crystalline key increased as it made contact with the surface. She removed the key as both doors swung away, opening into a large circular room.

The lighted trough had also activated a similar lighting apparatus in this room. Buck saw a large round room, roughly sixty feet in diameter. Along the walls were more recesses. These were not filled with artifacts and documents, but held large statues of seated figures, all over ten feet tall.

Columns stood about ten feet out from the walls, forming a smaller circle in the middle. The columns met a domed roof nearly twenty feet high. In the center of the dome was round transparent, crystalline material in a convex shape, forming what resembled a large lens. It was dark behind the lens. 'Probably another room above us,' thought Buck.

At the feet of the columns, the floor dropped away, forming a nearly forty-foot wide round pit that dropped straight down. Opposite their position, Buck noted two doorways, one shut and the other a smaller dark opening, about six or seven feet high, in the west side of the room.

"I think we need to head over and look for a way down" he said.

"Yes – let's look at that opening across the way," Kate replied.

The made their way around the right side of the room, looking at the statues as they went. "This is incredible," Buck said. "We do need to get your father in here. I wonder who these people were?"

"There's an entire history we don't know or understand here," Kate said. "Dad started to uncover it, and a lot of his peers gave him a hard time, claiming it was all waste of time and energy."

"Not anymore," Buck offered as they reached the smaller door. "I bet he'll have a heyday in here."

A faint sound, almost like thunder echoed from the ceiling above. Buck's mind immediately went to the expected German attack. "We don't have much time."

Kate's expression fell. "The Germans are here?"

"I think that noise was an explosion up above. Asad has most likely engaged with Krause's men by now. Let's hurry."

The sun had set on Giza. A small battle raged in the ruins near the Sphinx, the sound of gunfire echoing through the crumbled walls. Smoke obscured the fading light, limiting visibility. Asad's men had managed to slow the German convoy down, but were not able to stop them.

Only a short time before, Ibrahim's team had attacked the convoy to kick off the battle. The surprise attack was not as effective as the previous night's raid. A truck with an MG42 mounted in the back was enough to drive Ibrahim's strike team back while Krause's men pushed towards the Sphinx.

Hakeem, anticipating the eventual German advance, had placed his men in well-covered positions around the ruins to the front and north of the monument, which allowed them to cover the entrance to the Hall of Records.

At first, Hakeem's strategy worked. As they focused on protecting the entrance to the underground temple, a contingent of Krause's men had worked their way around the back side of the Sphinx to flank the Arab fighters. The German attack from the side disrupted Hakeem's men, forcing the survivors to take cover in the ruins.

As this played out, Asad had gathered a group of fourteen men to attack the Germans from the East, but he knew a frontal attack in the open would be ineffective. The German's flanking maneuver had done too much damage, and they had started to engage Hakeem's men in close-quarter fighting within the ruins. The Nazi remnant now had the advantage of cover within the ruined temple, and Asad's small troop would have to attack in the open as they advanced from the Village outskirts.

As Asad considered his options, the flanking Germans made way for Krause and two of his lieutenants to search for an entrance into the chambers below the Sphinx. It only took moments for them to find the blocked access shaft in the rear. Krause, unconcerned about preserving the integrity of the history around him, simply blasted the obstruction away with dynamite, revealing a network of air shafts. This was the thunder that Buck heard while exploring the circular temple.

Buck's light revealed steps leading down to the left, following the outside curvature of the chamber walls. The stairs curved around to the south side of the circular pit, then stopped at a small landing that opened into another room that was almost an exact copy of the room above. The ancient lighting system they had activated at the entrance was functioning here as well, revealing the same arrangement of columns and statues surrounding a forty-foot wide pit. The landing led to another stair, also following along the outside of the curved walls.

Buck judged they were probably at the south side of the chamber, about twenty feet below where they had started their descent. He started down the second flight of steps, this time opening into the East side of the pit, revealing another room with a similar layout. They continued down the narrow steps again.

This same pattern repeated two more times, until a final landing opened into the West side of the circular pit.

Now eighty feet down, the central chamber was different than the previous three. The ancient lighting system was still working, illuminating the lowest floor of the circular temple. This room also had the columns surround an opening in the floor, but now filled with water. There were no statues.

To their right, a narrow stone walkway extended into the center of the pool. The walkway connected to a twenty-foot wide stone circle, forming a ring with a smaller pool of water inside it. The walkway and ring were both about five feet wide.

On the outside edge of the ring stood four fifteen-foot-tall obsidian-colored pylons, each one placed on the four points of the compass. The pylons were decorated on all sides with inlaid symbols that appeared to be made of a clear crystalline material. Two small pedestals about four feet high marked the Northwest and Southeast compass points. Inside the ring was a smaller pool of dark water, roughly ten feet in diameter. Buck felt this inner pool of water was the focal point of the room.

"I think we're here," Kate said quietly. "This must be it – The Osiris Tomb."

"Yeah. This looks important." Buck looked around and noticed the walls in this lower chamber were decorated with a series of reliefs. Kate saw where his attention was directed, and shone at the walls.

Kate started to follow them clockwise around the room. The reliefs were presented as one continuous work, one blending into the next. Buck walked behind her, studying the ancient pictures.

The first relief depicted a map with land masses and bodies of water that were vaguely familiar to Buck, but he couldn't quite place them. The next image appeared to show an ancient town or city surrounded by mountains, with tall structures and people walking the streets. Above the city floated a depiction of two obelisk-shaped items with a round object between them. The third was another very recognizable map that appeared to show trade routes all over the world. A fourth relief focused on a man holding an object resembling an obelisk keystone over his head, while a large partially-built structure filled the background.

Next was another map, similar to the one with trade routes, but it showed a gigantic wave washing over the map, followed by a scene of people rebuilding ruined cities or towns. Each subsequent relief alternated between an apparent geographic image and a depiction of an event. The last relief was of the great sphinx, sitting behind a door. Buck recognized it as the hidden entrance they had discovered at the feet of the Sphinx.

They had walked three-quarters of room's circumference, when Buck realized what we was looking at. "This is telling a story isn't it?"

"Yes. It seems to be a depiction of events, showing us where the builders of this temple came from, and leading right up to the building of this temple."

"Incredible," Buck replied.

"Indeed it is," said a deep voice with a distinct German accent. Krause and two armed men holding MP-40 machine guns stepped out of the stairwell. Krause had his Mauser pistol aimed at them. "Now, my friends, you are going to help me recover the Covenant Stone."

Chapter 8 – The Osiris Tomb, Giza Plateau - Egypt

Once again, Asad found himself desperately praying for reinforcements. Only a few minutes before, his small band of fighters charged the men surrounding the ruins. He knew it was a desperate move before they made it, but he could not leave anyone to fight and possibly die alone against the Nazi remnant. Hakeem and his men were in dire need of help, and Asad could no longer wait for Jock and Emmitt to bring the help they needed.

They charged the German line, surprising them from behind. They opened fire midway through the charge, breaking the German ranks. Straggling Nazis fell to Arab knives and short swords. To Asad's surprise, they successfully fought their way into the ruins to Join Hakeem's group.

Hakeem's men had largely held up and had few losses, thanks to the cover provided by the ruined temple. Asad's arrival energized the men and disrupted the German forces enough to force them to change tactics; as he hoped, the Arabs were no longer surrounded, and were now engaging in close-quarter fighting. Asad's men excelled at this, and initially, the tactical shift was enough to give him hope they would prevail.

German rifles had limited use in hand-to-hand fighting, and most of the Arabs were armed with knives and pistols, which worked well in close quarters. The Nazi remnant took a large round of losses right away, as Asad's men took out between ten and fifteen men. Asad and Hakeem exchanged nods as both men started to believe tide had been turned.

Their eyes met when Hakeem registered a look of surprise. A bloody hole appeared in his chest and he slumped to the ground, resting against a broken wall.

Asad's hopes were soon dashed as he realized the German numbers were just too great. A second wave of former Nazi fighters replaced the fallen Germans. If the opposing forces had been equal in number, the fight would be in the Arab's favor. However, the Germans simply outnumbered his men three to one. Asad took cover and prayed for his men.

Inside the underground temple, Krause held his Mauser to Kate's back, a cold, silent smile cracking his burnt face. He stared at Buck, whose hands were now tied behind his back. Buck was backed up against a column near the pool, with one of the two Nazis pointing an MP-40 in his direction. His weapons were piled near the wall next to the chamber entrance. The other Nazi henchmen picked up their utility bags, and started rifling through them.

"I knew we would meet again, Captain Haggard. This time, you don't have the luxury of heavy artillery to cover your escape." He turned the burned side of his face towards Buck. "This is quite painful. I plan on making you suffer."

"Looks like an improvement to me," Buck wanted to goad the Nazi into talking. He could just get his right forefinger into one of the knots at his wrist. It wasn't much, but it was a start. He started trying to force his finger into the knot. "Your face never was much to look at."

"I will admit that you put on a brave show, Captain. But I don't think you are leaving here alive."

'Keep talking jackass,' Buck thought to himself. ' I'll get these knots yet.' Out loud, he said, "Where's the fun in that? Shoot me and leave me here in an abandoned temple? I expected a little more out of you."

Krause ignored the taunt and looked around the circular room, with its domed roof more than eighty feet overhead. "Look around you, Captain. Can you imagine what this was like, thousands of years ago? This isn't just a temple; it's a time capsule, a library of information on civilizations, kings, and generals that rose and fell before our known history.

"And as priceless as the texts and artifacts in this temple may be, they all pale next to the power contained within the Covenant Stone. The power to build or destroy at will. The power we need to launch the Fourth Reich."

"I think you're chasing a myth, Wilhelm," Buck said. "You're in for a big disappointment."

"We will see, Captain Haggard."

Krause scowled and turned his attention to Kate and spoke in a quiet, rasping voice. "Karl here will find your crystal keys. If you are as smart as your father, you will show me how we use them." Kate started ahead silently, not wanting to show the Nazi any sign of fear or compliance.

Karl produced the two keystones, still wrapped in rags. He unwrapped them, the blue-white glow illuminating his face. Krause watched as a look that could only be described as lustful crept into his burnt face.

The knot in Buck's rope was slowly loosening. He had to keep Krause busy, buy time. "You don't even know how to use those things. And even if you figure it out, what is it you think this stone will give you? Money to raise a new army? Make you the next Furher?"

Krause laughed. "We don't need a new Furher, Yankee, nor do we need money. We need a weapon, and a symbol to build our new movement upon. I want you to see us take the stone before you die." He waved his Mauser towards his other henchmen. "Dieter, if he keeps talking, cut his tongue out."

Dieter, a big, meaty looking man, smiled and grunted his pleasure with the order. He walked over, eying Buck like an animal meant to be slaughtered. "You won't need this much longer," he growled, taking the Reds cap. "Baseball is the only worthwhile thing Americans have invented," he said in an almost civilized tone. Dieter tossed the cap towards Buck's weapon and satchel, presumably to claim as a trophy later.

Buck bit his tongue, and continued working on the knotted rope as he watched Krause take one of the keystones from Karl. As he touched the crystal object, he felt the subtle humming vibration that emanated from it. "Incredible," Krause whispered with a cold smile. He holstered his pistol and faced Kate. "Now tell us how to use this."

Kate started to back away as Krause grabbed her by the arm. He led her, along with his henchman onto the stone walkway. Kate shot a look at Buck. He nodded, wanting her to comply. He needed her to keep Krause's attention as he continued to work on the ropes.

Kate picked up on Buck's intentions. She calmly pointed to the pedestals on the northwest and southeast sides of the inner walkway. "The keystones should go there," she said. "I don't know if it matters which pedestals they go with."

Krause took a position by the southeastern pedestal, his back to Buck. He motioned for Karl to go to the opposite pedestal.

Kate said quietly, "If these work like the entrance, there should be a slight depression where the key sits."

Krause looked at the pedestal in front of him and wiped centuries of dust from it. Like the pedestal in the front of the Sphinx, there was a rectangle etched into the surface. Krause slowly lowered the crystal key to it, lining the depression up with the base of the key. He looked across the pool to Karl, who followed suit. As Karl made contact with the second pedestal, both Keys emitted a burst of blue light. The light burst faded into a faint blue glow.

A subtle vibration emanated from the walkway around the pool. The water in the center pool started to foam and bubble, a warning that something was quickly ascending from the depths below.

Buck felt his ropes loosening as we worked harder to get his hands free. He knew that whatever was happening could provide the distraction he needed. Dieter's attention was on the foaming pool.

The crystalline symbols on the pylons began to glow. Whatever energy was contained in the keystones was also present in the pylons. A hundred feet above them, the lens-like fixture in the domed ceiling suddenly projected a beam of focused moonlight straight down into the center pool, highlighting the foaming disruption. Water spilled over the walkway as a large black object erupted from the depths.

It took Buck a moment to make sense of what he saw. A round black stone platform surfaced, supporting a large obsidian sarcophagus resting at a 45-degree angle. The sarcophagus faced the southwest side of the chamber, directly in line with the walkway. The ancient coffin bore no resemblance to any Egyptian sarcophagus; it was smooth, almost cylindrical in design. At its top were two black stone wings extending straight up. The lid was made of a semi-translucent crystalline substance similar to the keystones. The ancient casket dwarfed Krause and Kate. The underlying vibration around them stopped just as the moonlight struck the crystal lid, suffusing it with a blue-white glow.

Everyone in the chamber was struck silent with awe, unsure of what to expect.

Buck regained his composure and renewed his efforts to pull his hands free, realizing he only had moments to make a move. As he started pulling one of the knots loose, Krause motioned Karl to the front of the huge sarcophagus. Karl walked around the platform and stood next to his leader, placing Kate's satchel on the ground at their feet

The light coming from the symbols embedded in the pylons began to increase in intensity, and the glowing sarcophagus lid split down the middle. The two halves slid to either side, revealing a massive figure reclined in deaths endless slumber. The body was at least nine feet tall and completely wrapped in dull silver-grey metallic bands, resembling a futuristic mummy. The giant's hands were resting on its chest, cupped around a black baseball-sized stone.

Krause looked to Karl, who took the cue and stepped onto the platform. The Nazi henchman reached forward and touched the black stone. Just as he made contact, his eyes shot wide as if he had touched a live wire. Smoke exhaled from his mouth and nostrils. He tried to pull back, but was frozen by intense pain throughout his body. His hand started to turn black and suddenly light shot from his eyes, nose, and mouth as he was incinerated from the inside out. Karl's skin blacked and cracked, and within seconds, his ghastly, burnt husk collapsed on the platform and rolled off into the dark water.

The Nazi soldier stepped onto the platform...

Kate looked around, and started slowly backing away, inching down the walkway back to the outer part of the chamber as Krause grabbed her arm, forcing her towards the platform. He pulled his Mauser from its holster, and pointed it at Kate. "How do we retrieve the stone?" Krause hissed.

Kate shot a look over at Buck, who nodded slightly. 'Keep him busy' he thought. 'Just a little more time'. Buck shot a glance up at his beefy guard Dieter. His attention was consumed by the scene in front of him.

Kate took a breath and gathered her wits. She glared at Krause and said, "If you want the stone, then let go of my arm you son of a bitch." She stepped around Krause to get to each of the two pedestals, picking up the crystal keystones.

"You goose-stepping morons really aren't very smart, are you?" She decided if she had to play along, she was going to antagonize him every step of the way. Krause scowled, but accepted the verbal abuse. Buck smiled as he heard Kate's defiance.

Kate carried a keystone in each hand, and stepped slowly onto the central platform. She approached the massive coffin and raised her hands, the back sides of the crystals facing the gigantic mummified corpse. She had to step onto the lower edge of the black sarcophagus in order to get the Keys close to the stone cupped in its hands.

When she had the Keys about six inches away from the black stone, she felt something pulling on the keystones, as if a magnetic force were drawing them close to the stone. The black, rough-edged stone suddenly levitated and shot up between the keystones, almost violently causing them to slam together, capturing the stone in the cavity carved into the back of each Key. Kate managed to maintain a grip on the crystals, now held together by a force that she did not understand.

She stepped back off of the coffin, pausing on the edge of the platform and looking at the crystalline container with the Covenant Stone in the center. She felt it producing a vibration, as if it held some enormous power that ached to be released. As she examined the assembled object, faint markings on opposite sides were slowly becoming visible, as if the Stone's energy had catalyzed some ancient invisible text.

"Now bring it to me." Krause's voice interrupted her before the markings were fully materialized. As Kate complied, she realized the crystalline coffin lids were closing. She jumped back onto the circular walkway next to Wilhelm Krause just as the vertical lids slammed closed. The shaft of light from the roof faded out as the platform began to drop into the murky depths. It was gone almost as quickly and violently as it had appeared.

Krause picked up the satchel with his left hand as he kept the Mauser trained on Kate. As she dropped the assembled Covenant Stone into the bag, Buck slipped his right hand from the ropes. 'Now or never,' he thought.

The smoky air stank of gunpowder. Asad and his remaining men had taken cover in the center of the temple ruins, surrounded by the Nazi remnant. He had resigned himself to believing Jock had failed, and most likely Buck and the girl would not survive.

He had conferred with his men and they unanimously voted to charge the Germans and take as many as possible to their grave. All agreed that the Nazi remnant must be confronted no matter the cost. Every one of Asad's men recalled the Nazi occupation a few years ago – All had experienced personal loss or pain from it.

Asad and his men steeled themselves for a final, fatal charge when they heard the whine of incoming ordnance, mortar fire from the East. A sudden explosion rocked the sand just outside of the ruins, resulting in German cries of surprise and confusion.

Asad prayed it was the help they needed, but still refused to get his hopes up as he pulled his short sword from his belt and gave the signal to charge.

They directed their ferocity at the nearest German target, a short sprint across a moonlit courtyard within the ruins. The Arab men expected a wave of bullets to meet them; instead they saw Germans scattered and taking cover from something in the opposite direction. The confused German soldiers found themselves caught between Asad's small band and a larger, well-armed company of men dressed in black and wielding rifles and swords.

At the forefront, Asad made out Jock firing a handgun with a rifle slung across his back. The large red-headed warrior was wading into the fray with a ferocity that surprised Asad. At his side was a large dark-haired man he had never seen before, carrying an automatic pistol in each hand. Asad realized this must be the Armenian named Aram Avakian, leading the Sons of Seth into battle.

The surprised Nazi foot soldiers started to scatter, seeking shelter from the new threat. The Sons of Seth spread themselves out, working their way into the ruins in search of the rest of the German forces.

Jock ran to Asad, followed by Aram. "My God, they hit you hard. I'm sorry we couldn't get here faster…"

Asad grasped Jocks shoulder. "You are here now, so we have a chance. Let's find the rest of these rats."

"Yes," Jock agreed. "Any sign of Buck and Kate?"

Asad shook his head. "They disappeared underneath the Sphinx just before the attack. I'm sure Krause has made his way in after him by now."

Aram's face betrayed his concern. "We must make sure that whoever comes out, the Stone will remain safe."

"Don't give up on Buck yet," Jock countered. "He doesn't quit."

Dieter stood by the pool, still focused on the strange spectacle he had just witnessed. His back was to Buck, who quietly dropped the ropes to the floor. Buck quietly stepped behind Dieter, tapping him on his left shoulder. As the Nazi turned around, his face met a solid right hook. As Dieter staggered back into the pool, Buck turned and sprinted back towards the chamber entrance, jumping headfirst towards his gear.

Krause slung Kate's satchel over his shoulder and grabbed her from behind, pointing his Mauser towards her temple. "Haggard!" he shouted, "Don't be a fool!"

Buck claimed his shotgun. In one fluid motion he rolled to his feet and pumped the foregrip to chamber a round, when he caught sight of six red shells next to his gear. The magazine was empty!

Krause laughed, shaking his head. "You're out of luck, my friend. If you try to follow me, she's dead."

As Krause stepped off the walkway, Dieter pulled himself from the pool, his broad face red with anger. Krause looked at Dieter, admiring his henchman's rage. He decided to taunt Buck. "If it makes you feel any better, I won't need her after Dieter finishes with you."

Krause pushed Kate towards the chamber entrance as Dieter launched himself towards Buck. The heavy-set German moved surprisingly fast.

Buck braced himself for Dieter's charge. He squared his stance with Dieter's charge, bent his knees and dropped his center of gravity. He flipped his shotgun around so the stock pointed at Dieter's midsection, and gripped the gun with both hands.

As Dieter closed in, Buck leaned forward and brought the stock of his gun up into Dieter's groin as hard as he could. Dieter dropped like a rock, and before he could hit the ground Buck brought the stock back across the German's head, stunning the large Nazi.

Buck knew he only had seconds to end this. Dieter hit the ground, but was already struggling to get back up. Buck pulled the operating handle back, opening the breach in the gun's receiver. He grabbed a twelve gauge shell off the floor and slapped it into the receiver.

Dieter lunged a second time, and took the full blast of the Browning shotgun to his chest. His body tumbled backwards with a dull thud as the blast echoed around the chamber.

Buck looked around. Krause and Kate were gone. He grabbed his gear, slinging the shotgun bandolier across his chest. Buck picked up the shells from the ground and quickly reloaded the Ranger with the five remaining shells. Next he fished the flashlight out of the satchel. Last, he picked up his lucky Reds cap, still lying where Dieter tossed it moments before. He put it on his head, pulling it down in his subtle display of determination.

Buck pointed his light towards the chamber exit and sprinted after Kate and her captor. He could hear them somewhere above, presumably making their way back towards the Hall of Records and the entrance.

As Buck reached the top level of the circular temple, he saw the large doors across the room slam shut. Buck ran around the pit, only to find the doors locked. Without the Keystones, the door was locked. He had to find another way out.

Buck stopped and scanned his surroundings. Looking back towards the stairwell passage, he remembered the second door. 'It's worth a try,' he thought. Buck jogged back to the doorway next to the stairwell passage and looked at the heavy wooden slab blocking his way.

Buck used his light to examine the door. It had a sliding bolt on the right side. Buck pulled the bolt, forcing it through centuries of accumulated dust. He put his shoulder to the door, slowly forcing it open. The ancient lighting system didn't operate in here. Buck used his flashlight and saw a tunnel leading ahead of him into the dark. A few feet ahead, he saw the tunnel intersected at right angles by another passage leading off in either direction. Buck took the right hand tunnel and was relieved to see it curve to the right, following the perimeter of the ancient temple.

After Krause pushed the massive inner temple doors shut, he grabbed Kate's arm, pulling her through the hall of Records. He ran to the north side of the chamber and stopped as he saw a rope piled in some rubble on the floor. In the ceiling above was a jagged hole, created by the Nazi's use of dynamite to clear a passage from the surface.

"Which way did you come in?" he growled. Kate was set to resist answering when she realized his exit had been compromised. She saw a chance to delay him and let Buck catch up.

Kate pointed ahead, and quietly said, "Up the small stairwell on the left, on the other end of the room." She hoped he wouldn't see through the lie.

Krause looked at her, studying her face. Without replying, he pulled her the length of the ancient library, stopping near the entrance. Darkness lay beyond the front door. Krause turned to the stairwell to their left, leading Kate up into the darkened passage. Krause fished a light from Kate's satchel to combat the heavy darkness of the stairwell. They reached a landing, where Kate was aware of several other passages running parallel to the ancient library below.

Krause instinctively pulled her up another steep flight of stairs, assuming up was the logical way out. They seemed to be heading up and over the Hall of Records, into the body of the Sphinx.

At the top of the steps they entered a small chamber. It was claustrophobic compared to the relative spaciousness of the Hall below. The walls on either side were lined with more jars, boxes and artifacts. There was no obvious door or passage except the one they had just come from.

"You bitch!" Krause muttered, realizing she had misdirected him. Krause whipped his light around, looking for an exit. Kate saw a series of small horizontal recesses carved into the far wall, forming a ladder leading up. A lever extended from the wall next to the recesses. She suddenly realized where they were. Kate decided to let Krause figure it out on his own, hoping it would delay them enough for Buck to catch up.

Her hopes were dashed when Krause grabbed the lever and pulled it down. A dry stone-on-stone grinding noise filled the chamber, as a round opening above the ladder opened up, allowing moonlight to illuminate the small chamber.

Buck sprinted up a steep flight of stairs, curving back to the east as far as he could tell. At the top of the stairs, the passage opened into a large circular room with nearly translucent floor. The room was surprisingly well lit. He could barely make out a room below when he realized he was probably standing on the same lens-like crystalline object that was in the vaulted ceiling of the Osiris Tomb.

To his left was a recess in the wall that appeared to be the source of the room's lighting. Buck realized that he was seeing moonlight shining in at an angle, striking the crystalline floor and reflecting light throughout the room. Buck moved closer, and saw that the recess was the bottom end of a shaft, sloping up and to the outside.

Buck studied the walls of the shaft. The angle was steep, but he thought he could manage it. With a little luck, he would be able to catch up to Krause outside the ancient temple.

Jock, Aram and Asad fought their way through the ruined temple. They had pushed through the temple and made their way to the neighboring Funerary Temple ruins. Aram surprised a small group of four Nazi soldiers taking cover in an enclosed passage leading up to the causeway. He immediately fired on them with his pistol, killing one. Asad pulled out his long curved knife and violently waded into them. Jock barely had time to fire on one before the Egyptian had already killed two of the soldiers.

The passage sloped upwards and ended in an open gateway. Jock and his companions followed the passage and found themselves on the raised causeway along the south side of the Sphinx. Jock stepped through the gate cautiously looking around. He looked to his right, where the Sphinx rested. The moon was bright, providing enough light for him to see The Sons of Seth, accompanied by what was left of the Arab forces, as they engaged the Nazi remnant in a skirmish at the base of the Sphinx. Bodies from both sides littered the ground.

Aram joined Jock, using the large blocks in the center of the causeway for cover. "We are starting to take them," he said. "We will need to find a way into the hall of Records soon."

Jock was about to respond when movement on top of the Great Sphinx's head caught his eye. "Look," he said, pointing to the top of the monument. "Someone is up there."

A large figure stood on top of the Sphinx, holding a leather satchel in his right hand and a handgun in his left. A smaller female figure slowly climbed out of a hole on top of the Sphinx as the larger man pointed his gun at her.

Jock's face fell. "It's Krause. And he has Kate."

Asad nudged Jock's arm. "Look to the back of the statue."

A figure was emerging on top of the Sphinx's back, near the far end of the monument. Jock could just make out a sawed-off pump shotgun in his hands. As the man stood up, he tugged on a worn red and blue baseball cap.

Jock nodded an acknowledgment to Asad, and holstered his pistol. He unslung his Lee Enfield no. 1 Mk III around and checked the magazine. As he readied his weapon, Jock quietly stated, "I told you Buck doesn't quit."

Buck emerged from the square shaft and looked around. He instantly realized that Jock had successfully brought reinforcements. Below him, Nazi soldiers were being pushed back on both sides of the Sphinx by Arab fighters accompanied by fighters dressed in black. Several pockets of hand-to hand fighting persisted on either side as the Nazis gave ground to the combined forces of Asad and Aram Avakian.

Buck saw Krause and Kate standing on top of the Sphinx.

Buck scanned the causeway wall to his right, and spotted three men near the temple gate. He could just make out Jock readying his rifle in the moonlight. Behind Jock stood Asad, and Buck assumed the third man to be Avakian.

As he continued to scan from his right, he saw Krause and Kate standing on top of the Sphinx's head. Buck started towards them, shotgun half raised as Krause acknowledged Buck's advance.

"Haggard! Stop where you are or I'll kill her."

Buck slowed his advance. "You're surrounded, Wilhelm. Let her go and we'll bring you in alive. Your men are losing, and you have nowhere to go."

Krause found the nerve to laugh. "I have the Stone, and I have your woman. Despite the failure of my soldiers, I think I have an advantage, my friend. I am going to walk away from here with the Stone, or she'll die where we stand." To emphasize his point, Krause pushed Kate in front of him, his Mauser pointed to her head. He held the satchel with the Stone in his right hand.

Buck stopped, his mind racing. Krause wasn't wrong. If confronted with a fight, he would almost certainly kill Kate. To make matters worse, if they let him walk away, he would still take her as a hostage, and possibly kill her once he was away. If Krause made it back down into the passages below, he could slip away for good.

Jock assessed the scene playing out in front of him. Buck had just surfaced from the back of the Sphinx, and had the Nazi's attention. Krause was unaware that Jock and his companions were watching the standoff unfold. The only hope they had of keeping Kate safe was to take Krause out before he could act on his threat. He steadied the Lee Enfield on the stone wall in front of him, and slowly adjusted the scope to bring Krause into view. His movements were very deliberate and cautious, taking care not to draw Krause's attention away from Buck

---

Buck knew his partner was covering Krause. He needed to keep the German focused on their confrontation, and find a way to keep Kate from harm.

Buck took a breath, put down the Ranger and held up his hands. "Okay, okay. Take the Stone Krause! I just want the girl. Let her go and you can walk away."

Krause shook his head. He still needed a distraction to escape. "I wish I could believe you, Haggard."

Kate looked back at Krause, her eyes widening with fear. Suddenly a loud *crack!* echoed through the air. Jock's Lee Enfield slammed a bullet into Krause's left shoulder, sending him reeling sideways.

Krause stumbled, but somehow maintained his footing. He shoved Kate in the back, sending her stumbling over the steep slope of the Sphinx's head. She turned as she fell and grasped the satchel with her right hand, pulling Krause forward. He landed on his stomach, a death grip on the satchel's handle. Kate was desperately clenching the bag, hanging on the steep headdress of the Sphinx, trying to find a foothold.

Buck sprinted forward, all of his attention now on Kate. Damn Krause and damn the Stone, he was going to catch Kate before she could tumble to the desert floor below.

Krause slowly brought his injured left arm up, still gripping the Mauser. Kate's grip slowly gave way in spite of her determination to hang on. A second shot struck Krause in his side as he lost the grip on the bag. Almost simultaneously, Kate's grip failed and she started sliding down the back side of the Sphinx's head.

Buck reached a spot just below Kate's trajectory. He braced himself to break her fall. Out of the corner of his eye, he saw the satchel tumble down the stone slope to his left.

Kate's weight hit Buck square in the chest as he collapsed backwards, absorbing the impact from her fall. He felt the wind push out of his lungs as their combine weight hit the rocky backbone of the Great Sphinx.

Buck sucked in air as he realized Kate was on top of him and alive. "Are you OK?" he asked.

Kate sat up. "Nothings broken, but I've had better days."

Buck scrambled to his feet, looking for his enemy. "Krause – where did he go?"

Kate sat up as Buck shouted over to his allies on the causeway, "Do you see him?"

"No," Jock shouted back." He seemed to just disappear. I think he went back down into the passageway on top. I'll see if we can get some men to go in after him."

Buck waved his acknowledgement as Kate looked around. "The Stone," she said. "It's out here somewhere."

"I think it fell down to the ground." Buck helped Kate up and walked back to pick up his shotgun. "Let's go down and look." Buck checked both side of the Sphinx, noting that the fighting on the ground had subsided.

The north side of the monument had a badly eroded surface, exposing the natural stone beneath. The moonlight provided good visibility as they found a path down to the ground. After they descended, Kate ran the length of the Sphinx until they stood beside massive shoulders of the mythical beast.

A brown leather satchel lay in the sand at the Sphinx's shoulder. Kate picked it up carefully and opened the flap. A faint blue-white glow escaped, illuminating her face. "It's intact," she said with a sigh of relief.

"So you have it," Buck said. "Now what are you going to do?"

Kate closed the flap and looked at Buck. "I don't know. You saw this thing fry that German, and how it levitated when I removed it from the sarcophagus. We really don't understand what this is."

"Yeah. It's also pretty clear that Krause and his bunch believe this is the key to reviving the Nazi war machine. It's not going to be safe in a museum."

Kate nodded, thinking about the implications of their discovery. As she contemplated the options, Buck noticed four figures approaching in the moonlight. It was Jock, Asad, Aram and Emmitt.

"Katie!" the Professor cried as he approached. "Are you OK?"

She looked up at the sound of her father's voice and replied, "We found it Dad. It's right here." She patted the bag, now hanging off her shoulder. Kate's expression turned serious. "You didn't get involved in the battle, did you?"

"No, Aram's men kept me safe in the village until the fighting subsided. They knew I was going to come looking for you sooner than later, so once they felt it was safe enough, they let me go - with a small contingent of bodyguards."

Aram clapped Emmitt's shoulder. "I would not forgive myself if I let my friend get hurt," he said with a rare smile. Aram turned to Buck, looking him up and down. "So you are the infamous Buck Haggard. Your appearance is exactly the way I imagined.

"We are sending a few men in to secure the temple and try to root out the Nazi leader. I will be honest, I don't expect to find him. There are tunnels all over this area, with many escape routes."

Buck nodded. "Something tells me we'll see him again anyway."

Emmitt turned his attention to the satchel. "Can I see it?" he asked.

Kate sat the bag down and slowly opened the top, allowing the relic's blue-white glow to escape. Kate put both hands in the bag, and slowly brought the assembled crystalline block out. The Covenant Stone was a dark mass buried in the center of the translucent Crystal. There were very faint traces of ancient writing that had appeared on opposite sides of the block.

The six of them stared for a moment, until Kate broke the silence. "I should put this away. It's extremely dangerous. Down in the Temple... I watched it burn a man from the inside out."

As she knelt to put the Covenant Stone away, Emmitt turned to Aram. "You and your men are sworn to protect this artifact from anyone who would abuse it, isn't that correct?"

"Yes," Aram replied. "That is partly what we are here for. You could also say we are sworn to protect mankind from itself. The temptation to abuse the power of this Holy object is too great."

Kate stood up, looking at Aram as she considered his reply. "Then you should take it." She extended the satchel out towards Aram. "We aren't ready for this yet."

As Aram took the satchel, Buck put a hand on her shoulder. "Are you sure? You and your father have spent a lot of time looking for this."

Kate put her hand over Bucks, and leaned into him. "Yes, I'm sure. It's the right thing to do."

Epilogue

Buck, Jock and Kate sat in Professor Carter's study. Buck was restless, trying to get comfortable sitting in front of Emmitt's large cherry desk. Three of the four walls were lined with shelves; all packed with books and maps, artifacts, folders full of papers, and various odds and ends collected from all over the world. One wall, to the left of the great desk, was a large picture window, looking out over the rural countryside. Emmitt's study was like the rest of his house –large, comfortable, and in need of a maid. Buck didn't mind the clutter. He looked out the window, taking in the telltale signs of fall through the glass.

Buck still wasn't used to the cool New York Autumn air – too many years in South America, not to mention his recent stint in the Middle East, had acclimated Buck to much warmer temperatures. The last couple of months back in the States had been some of the best he could remember, but not due to the weather. He and Kate had grown closer, and he could see a future with her.

If only he didn't have this nagging, restless feeling as if something from the past were going to show up and throw a monkey wrench into the mix. The fact that Professor Carter had asked the three of them to be here today didn't help to ease this feeling.

As they waited, Jock asked, "Kate, do you know what the Prof has on his mind? It's not like him to insist all of us gather on such short notice -" He stopped as Professor Carter entered the study.

Emmitt sat behind his massive desk. "Ah - - Good, you're here. I hoped you three would make it on time."

Kate spoke up, "Dad, what's going on? You seemed to have something serious on your mind when asked us to meet you here."

"Well, something serious is going on. Our old acquaintance Aram Avakian is on his way here, and we have something we need to tell you."

Buck frowned. "I have a bad feeling about this," he said quietly.

Emmitt raised eyebrows, considering the remark. "You may be justified, Buck. I do have to admit that I've been keeping in contact with our Armenian friend since we left Egypt, and have been helping him with some research related to the crystal keys and the Covenant Stone, and we do have something to share.

However, I think there is more that Aram wants from us, and I think we owe him a few minutes to hear what he has to say. He did save our bacon, after all."

"No question. He did just that. And if I have learned anything about people like him, there is always the expectation of a return favor, and it is rarely easy or safe. Hell, I even operated that way for a long time." Buck looked at Kate. "But I can't imagine living the rest of my life always owing and collecting favors. There are better things in life."

Kate looked at the floor and smiled as the sound of a doorbell echoed through the house. Emmitt stood up, and said, "I'll get that".

As he walked out of the study, Jock mumbled," Guess we'll find out soon enough."

A few minutes later, Emmitt walked in, followed by Aram Avakian. Aram was carrying a square wooden box with wrought iron handles on either side. The box was almost perfectly square, with ornate carvings on each side and top. Aram set the box on the floor near Emmitt's desk.

"Hello old friends," the Armenian offered. "I apologize for the intrusion, but I have some important news for you. And as you may have guessed, I have something to ask."

Buck, unable to shake old habits, decided to cut to the chase. "Hello Aram. Clearly we are in your debt. Let's hear what you have to say." He wanted to keep pleasantries short and sweet, and get the cards on the table.

Aram allowed a small smile to escape. He appreciated the American's direct manner. "We have learned a few things you may find surprising, and probably even interesting. First, let's talk about the Stone, and what we have learned in the last two months." Aram turned to Emmitt. "Professor, would you care to start?"

Emmitt cleared his throat. "Of course. As I said earlier, I stayed in touch with Aram and have been helping with some research related to our find. We've discovered a few things that may seem hard to believe, but I can assure you that what we have learned is true.

"In fact, I think that what we've been able to discern could change how we think about our forefathers, especially key figures in Biblical History."

Kate spoke up. "We already knew the Stone is connected to early Biblical mythology, especially Eden and Stories like the Tower of Babel. We even saw reliefs in the Osiris Tomb that possibly referenced events like the Flood and the Tower's collapse. Is that what you are talking about?"

"Not quite – it goes further than that. All of the research we had before our recent adventure was based on the Stone being used and lost after the Biblical Flood. In fact, it has surfaced in later events, just not in a way that was immediately recognizable. Let me ask you this; where did you find the second key?"

"Behind the worship complex on top of Jebel Al-Mahdbah, you know that," Kate said. "What's the connection?"

"I'm getting there," Emmitt replied. "Just hold that thought, and humor me as I walk through this.

"First, it's important to understand that the early stories we read in Genesis predate classical Egypt. An in-depth study of those stories reflect that there was probably a fairly advanced civilization that is only recalled through oral history and now remembered as the nearly allegorical stories we read in the Bible. There is a strong resemblance to early Mesopotamian stories. There is clearly some connection.

"As you know, I have a working theory that the people that predated classical Egypt were visited by travelers either from Mesopotamia or by a visitor common to both.

"The first mention I discovered of the Tablets and Covenant Stone was in Mesopotamian mythology, often referred to the 'Tablets of Destiny' or the 'Stone of Destiny'. I believe this was a description of the assembled object. It was captured by the Mesopotamian god Marduk, and subsequently used to secure his place as the ruler of the local 'gods'. In later mythology associated to this culture, the Stone was connected to great building projects such as the Tower of Babel.

"As I learned more, I found even more references to the Stone that suggested it had been around for a long time prior to this period. I don't want to bore you with too much detail, so let's say that it seems to have been used in whatever society we now remember as the Garden of Eden, and may even have been used to help survive the Flood recalled in Genesis.

"Anyway, the growth of a highly structured society in the fertile crescent happened after that flood event, with impressive results that are now remembered through stories like the Tower, and its destruction, and the subsequent 'scattering' of people to faraway lands.

"Not long after, in relative historical terms, we have the sudden appearance of the classical Egyptian civilization we are familiar with. The Giza complex is an early and impressive result of that growth spurt. In fact, we still don't understand the process or mechanism used to build the Pyramids."

The Professor took a pause and Jock asked "Are you saying the Stone was how the Great Pyramids and the Sphinx were built?"

"No, I'm not ready to say that. Regarding the Pyramids, we've pretty confidently dated them to Khafre's time. However, the Sphinx is potentially much older. It was also obvious that the Hall of Records was designed to use the keys for certain things – unlocking the front door, the entrance to the Tomb, and to call up and open the sarcophagus where Kate found the Stone. All indications are that the Sphinx, or at least its underlying structure, is quite a bit older.

"This all suggests the keys and the Stone were in use in various locations throughout the Middle East and Egypt more than five thousand years ago – Mesopotamia rose first, ostensibly with roots back almost six thousand years and with mythological connections to the Stone.

"Next, the Stone appears in Egypt, clearly associated with the Hall of Records, and the Egyptian civilization we all know springs up. That's probably enough exposition on theoretical prehistory of Egypt for now. But why do we find the crystal keys in places like Transjordan and Palestine?

"I think the answer is simple – they have been carried back and forth several times across several generations, and we actually have documented accounts and stories that illustrate this. One of them, in fact, is central to the Bible itself." Emmitt stopped, waiting for a reaction.

Buck shifted in his seat. "You're talking about the Exodus, aren't you?"

"Yes, I am. In fact, I believe you visited the very site where the Bible tells us that Israel's covenant with God was established."

"Yes, and so does Kate. Her argument is convincing too." The possible significance of Petra and the history that Kate had related while on top of Jebel Al-Mahdbah was not lost on Buck, but he wanted to hear more before he made any assumptions.

Jock jumped to the next question. "So how exactly are the keys and the Stone related to Mount Sinai? I get that the site at Petra might be the original Sinai, and that it was a place where the Keystones were hidden, but that doesn't mean they actually have anything to do with the Exodus."

Emmitt gestured towards Aram, "Oh but they do, and our friend here suspected this all along. As he studied the crystal objects we recovered, he was able to confirm his suspicions."

Aram took the queue to speak. "They are related because the keystones, as you call them, are not just keys. Nor were they originally referred to as such. They are more commonly known as the Tablets of the Covenant."

Buck's own interest in history finally took control of his reaction. "That's an incredible assertion. What in God's name led you to that conclusion?"

"A few things," Aram replied. "Please let me explain. The Sons of Seth have long held a theory that these objects were somehow associated to God's Covenant with man. Now we know how they relate.

"Our order has long held a doctrine that says that God's Law, the Covenant, was not written on Mt Sinai, but it was revealed and passed down to Moses there. It existed before him. I visited the cave on top of Jebel Al-Mahdbah. It is much older than even Moses' time, and was used as a place to hide the Covenant Stone and the tablets long before Moses arrived.

"The man-made cave on top of Mahdbah is actually laid out in a manner very similar to the desert tabernacle, as described in our Holy Scriptures. It may have actually provided the blueprint that Moses followed – and one that Solomon also followed when he had the First Temple built.

"Aside from that, I have two clear examples that support this artifact's connection to Moses. First, think about the account of Moses receiving the law on God's Mountain. Not only does the description in Exodus fit the mountain in Petra, the account says the commandments were written by God's finger.

"Next, when Moses descended and saw how the Israelites had sinned, he 'broke' the tablets and released a rain of destruction on the offending people.

"Let me explain these examples, taking the last one first. The Crystal blocks that hold the Covenant Stone serve two purposes; one, they act as a container of the Stone's properties, allowing one to safely hold and wield the Stone. If the blocks are suddenly pulled apart, it can release a dangerous burst of energy. You saw how the unshielded Stone can affect someone who is careless about handling it."

Buck and Kate exchanged glances. The mental image of the Germans soldier being burned from the inside out was still fresh in their minds.

"When Moses found his people had sinned, the Bible says he 'broke the tablets'. We think he split the two Crystal containers apart and released a devastating surge of energy."

"Okay. What about God 'writing' the commandment on the tablets"

"Ahh. That is the best evidence we have, and it proves we are right. Because last, but not in the least, we can see it with our own eyes."

"The markings, the ones that appeared when all three parts were assembled!" Kate exclaimed.

Emmitt smiled, "Yes, they are the Decalogue. This certainly challenges our traditional perception of the Ten Commandments.

"Aram, would you mind bringing it out?"

Aram opened the ornate box and carefully lifted a black cloth-covered object out. He set it on Emmitt's desk, and removed the cloth covering. A faint glow fell on their faces. The Blue-white Crystal held the dark-colored Covenant stone in its center, obscured by the Crystal and its inexplicable glow. On two opposite sides, five lines of dark writing were clearly visible, embedded just below the clear surface.

Emmitt continued. "The ancient script that appeared is a form of text that has very strong similarities with proto-Sinaitic script. In fact, we suspect it's an unknown root language predating both Egyptian Hieroglyphic and Semitic written languages. Moses was undoubtedly educated based on his position within the Egyptian ruling family, and may have even had access to the Hall of Records. If that's the case, some education on older, obscure languages is a strong possibility."

"You actually deciphered it?" Kate asked.

Emmitt smiled. "With the help of some documents recovered from the temple you discovered. The writing lays out the ten basic guidelines for societal interaction. Each guideline closely corresponds to the Decalogue as presented in the Bible.

"It's highly likely that it was at Mahdbah that the Stone and Tablets were 'assembled' and God's outline for living as a society was revealed to the Hebrews as they fled Egypt. The violent storms on Sinai that are described in the Bible could potentially be explained as a by-product of the Stone as well.

Kate stood and moved closer. She leaned in to examine the mysterious text, looking for familiar markings or patterns that would help her understand the text.

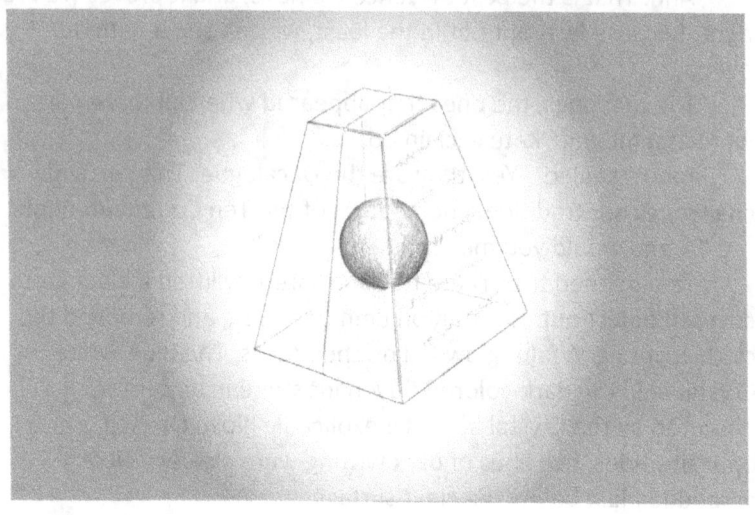

The Covenant Stone Assembled

Buck followed, questions spilling out in spite of himself. "How is it formed? What is the catalyst for making the writing appear?"

"We think the Stone causes it to become visible. I suspect the Stone was kept at Mahdbah until Moses came along – he may have even been aware it was there to begin with. Sinai, or Mahdbah as it's called now, had a reputation for storms and strange ecological behavior. The presence of the Crystal Tablets does not seem to cause that phenomenon, but the Stone itself does."

Buck thought a moment. "All of this implies that the Stone has been passed around all over that region. It wasn't always in the so-called Osiris Tomb, and that may in fact be a relatively recent resting place."

Aram nodded once in agreement. "We will never fully know where and how the Stone and tablets passed from hand to hand. We are sure that the Hebrews had it for a long time. I believe the Stone itself was probably taken back to Egypt between Solomon and Manasseh's reigns, about the time the Ark of the Covenant also disappeared. The two Crystal tablets were likely hidden at the same time, one near the Dead Sea, the other in the hidden shrine on God's Mountain. It appears that whoever hid them wanted to ensure the objects could not be easily assembled. And for good reason. We all know this either contains or channels a powerful energy that may be easily abused."

"What about the Ark, the golden chest used to carry the Decalogue?" Buck asked. "How does that figure in? Or does it?"

Emmitt responded with eagerness. His passion for the subject matter was clear. "The significance of the Ark has two sides: On one hand, it was a symbol of man's relationship with God, but by itself, it was just a box covered with gold.

"One the other hand, it contained the Crystal tablets and the Stone. It's entirely possible that a wooden box covered with a highly conductive metal could serve as a vessel to help control the power in the Stone.

"Beyond that, we aren't sure what it really was, where it might be, or what role it really played in how the Hebrews used it with the Stone. That is a mystery all by itself."

Buck looked at the Holy object in front of him. "I truly appreciate the knowledge here. It's staggering to think we are looking at the actual Tablets of the Ten Commandments. And it's clear that these tablets, along with the Stone, are also too dangerous for anyone to possess."

Buck turned to look at Aram. "And that's exactly why we turned it over to you, The Sons of Seth. So why bring this back to us now? What else is going on?"

Aram covered the Stone as he responded. "This is not the only Holy artifact that exists in the world. It may be the most well-known and perhaps even one of the most powerful, if not *the* most powerful. But it is not the only one.

"And as you know, we did not find the Nazi leader Krause. Despite his injuries, he managed to evade us at Giza."

"Yes." Buck wasn't surprised when he originally heard that Krause escaped. The punch line was coming.

"We need your help. There are other artifacts that are best described as 'companion' objects to the Covenant Stone in other parts of the world. And the same evil that came after this one is still looking for the others.

"Wilhelm Krause has been seen in South America, and we believe he is close to finding another such object that is hidden in the Amazon. We know you have extensive experience in the jungle. We are committed to stopping his new Nazi movement, but we need you to help us."

There it was – the proverbial monkey wrench. Buck looked at Kate and Jock. Jock's expression was clear; If Buck was in, he was in. Kate took a deep breath, and then looked Buck in the eyes. "You have to help, but not alone. I'm in too."

Buck knew she was right. He nodded, and turned back to face Emmitt and Aram Avakian. "When do we start?"

Afterword

Now that this is written down, and I am close to publishing, I felt it necessary to say a few additional things about the story and especially, the setting and the liberties I have taken with some real locations. Obviously, the story is fantasy, but I wanted to root in a couple of recognizable locations, primarily Petra and the Giza complex (which, in my view, includes the Saqqara Necropolis as well as the Great Pyramids and the Sphinx).

I'll address what is on my mind in the order it is presented in the story. First, the Dead Sea locale; En Gedi is a real settlement, but I have never been there. I was unable to find much information about the settlement circa 1946. I took broad liberties with that as a landing and docking point for the Goose. The idea for the caves is grounded in the Qumran region near the north end of the Dead Sea, but the cliffs and cave in my book are entirely fictional. My last comment on this particular geography is that I played pretty loose with the location of Sodom.

Petra is obviously a real place, as is Jebel Al-Mahdbah. In 1927, archeologist Ditlef Neilson did indeed propose this mountain to be the actual site where Moses received the Law from God. I have never read his book making the proposal, as it seems to be impossible to find a copy in English (I've tried). However, I have been there, and I truly believe that mountain is a special place.

Kate's theory about the Exodus route more or less following the "king's highway" is based on my own research, and I believe it to be a reasonable possibility.

And next, the Sphinx. I relied on more than a few "fringe theory" ideas about that ancient monument. These ideas have been circulated since alleged psychic Edgar Cayce claimed to have visions of a great temple under the Giza complex. Today, there are still lots of ideas and speculation about underground tunnels and temples at Giza. So far, there is no tangible proof that any of it is true…. but you never know.

As for the idea of the Covenant Stone itself – this is entirely my own fantasy, largely rooted in the idea that the things we read from our forefathers may not really be well understood by modern mankind. I'll leave you with this thought. I encountered it in BAR magazine as I was wrapping up the editing of this story:

"...Even though Yahweh is not bound to human limits, he condescended to mankind deferring to human expectations of divinity. ... God did not try to change the beliefs of the people before engaging them, but instead respected human frailty and human notions of the divine, inverting or modifying those beliefs to teach humanity new ideas about himself."

Quote from David A Falk, Biblical Archeology Review, May 2021, "The Ark of the Covenant in its Egyptian Context"
www.biblicalarchaeology.org/daily/biblical-artifacts/artifacts-and-the-bible/the-ark-of-the-covenant-in-its-egyptian-context

David Falk's article is not relevant to my story, but this quote is a concept that I like. This world, and its creator, is much bigger than we are. Once in a while I think it's good to be reminded of that. Maybe we need to be willing to accept that we don't – and can't – know everything.

Jim Cooper
Marysville, Ohio
September 2021

About the Author

Jim Cooper (1967-TBD) lives and works in Marysville Ohio. Jim grew up in rural southern Ohio, and after attending college joined the United States Air Force and finished his formal education. Jim has always been an avid student of history, a fan of classic cars, and fascinated by adventure and science fiction stories.

During his military career Jim was also fortunate enough to travel around the world, where he made a point to learn as much as he could about the many places he visited.

After his service in the military, Jim came home to Ohio, where he and his wife Kathy raised two sons and a daughter.

Jim now uses his own unique combination real-world history, experience, fringe theory and fantasy to craft his stories. He and Kathy continue to travel and learn about the amazing world we live in. *The Covenant Stone* is his first published effort.